I only said "yes" so that they'd like me

Dr. Celia Banting

WIGHITA PRESS

Requests for permission to make copies of any part of the work should be mailed to the following address:

Wighita Press
P.O. Box 30399
Little Rock, Arkansas, 72260-0399

www.wighitapress.com

This is a work of fiction. Names of characters, places, and incidents are products of the author's imagination and are used fictitiously and are not to be construed as real. Any resemblance to actual events, locales, organizations, or persons, living or dead, is purely coincidental.

Library of Congress Cataloging-in-Publication Data

Banting, Celia
I Only Said "Yes" So That They'd Like Me/
Dr. Celia Banting – 1st Edition
p. cm.
ISBN 0-9786648-1-7 (paperback)

1. Therapeutic novel   2. Suicide prevention   3. Bullying
4. Self-esteem

Library of Congress Control Number: 2006928585

Layout by Michelle VanGeest
Cover production by Luke Johnson

Printed by Dickinson Press, Grand Rapids, Michigan, USA

Issues addressed in this book:

Suicide prevention

Social masks

Stereotyping

In-groups and out-groups

Body Dysmorphic Disorder

Negative family dynamics

The role of marijuana upon behaviour

Coping with bullying

The emotional consequences of casual sex

Losing and regaining self-respect

Developing and maintaining friendships

Teamwork

Identifying talents and perceiving self-worth

Exploring attitudes and personal Frame of Reference

Self-esteem and affirmations

Guided imagery techniques

Discerning human attractiveness

Also by Dr. Celia Banting...

I Only Said I Had No Choice

I Only Said I Couldn't Cope

I Only Said I Didn't Want You Because I Was Terrified

I Only Said I Was Telling the Truth

. . . .

Available after April 2007...

I Only Said I Wanted To Kill Myself; I Didn't Really Mean It

I Only Said I Wasn't Hungry

I Only Said It Didn't Hurt

I Only Said I Could Handle It, But I Was Wrong

I Only Said Leave Me Out of It

Dedicated to Erica Elsie,
and all those who suffer at the hands of bullies

Acknowledgments

My grateful thanks go to my proofreader and typesetter, Michelle VanGeest, who frees me from my dyslexic brain, and replaces my mother's voice. Thanks to Bev, my stray-word spotter, too. I thank my dear brother, Steve, for his computer expertise, and my wonderful husband, Des, for the inspiration and support he gives me. Thank you to Luke and Sam for their faith, inspiration and talent. Thank you to my dear friend Vicki for her guiding sense of style.

Thank you to all my psychotherapy tutors and colleagues at the Metanoia Institute, London, for teaching me about human nature, psychopathology, growth and recovery.

I thank the good Lord for giving me a lively imagination, and I also thank my parents for moving to the Isle of Wight, "the land that bobs in and out of view, depending upon the sea mist."

Chapter One

I hate Mondays and I hate school. I pull the covers over my head and try to ignore Mom shouting at me to get up.

"Melody, will you *please* get up, you're going to make me late for work."

She yanks the covers off me and I feel a blast of cold air hit my body, which is curled up trying to keep warm. I snatch them back over me and cuss under my breath, hoping she doesn't hear me.

"Okay, okay," I say, trying to contain the irritation I feel, but as Buster, my black Labrador, jumps onto my bed and starts to lick my face, I can't stay mad for long.

I hug him as he washes my face to the point where I feel that I don't need a shower anymore. I don't know how I'd cope without him. Living in this house is like being alone in a crowd. There's Mom and Dad who bark at each other, if they can be bothered to speak at all, and there's my twin brother, Danny, who is so wrapped up in his skateboard that he doesn't do anything but grunt at everyone. The only one I get any attention from is Buster, so as he licks me and I smell his doggy breath, I hold on to him tightly and tell him I love him.

"Hurry up," Mom shouts, as she passes my door again, "Get up, or you'll have to walk to school."

I don't care, in fact I'd rather walk to school so that the kids don't see the car she drives and rip me to pieces all day about how poor we are.

Danny beats me to the shower and so I try to snuggle back down into my bed with Buster, pulling the covers over us, but he struggles to be free and cold air surrounds me, forcing me to get up and put some clothes on. It's no good being the last one in the shower because the water's cold by then, so I forget it, spray deodorant on myself and get dressed without washing. Finally Danny comes out of the bathroom and I can get in there to clean my teeth.

I stare into the mirror. I hate it that I look so much like my mom. I think my mom is the ugliest woman I've ever seen, even though she spends hours trying to hide her hooked nose, sunken, piggy eyes and thin lips with loads of makeup; it doesn't make any difference as far as I can see.

I put toothpaste on my toothbrush and start scrubbing, staring into the mirror, hating my own sunken piggy eyes and hooked nose. I have my dad's lips and for that I'm grateful. I scrub and scrub with a venom that reflects my anger that Danny, a boy at that, doesn't look anything like Mom; he's got beautiful eyes with lashes to die for, blonde hair, Dad's chiselled nose and full lips. If there's a God, why did He do this to me? Doesn't He know how hard it is to be a girl and not be pretty? Why did He give Danny what He should have given me?

I spit into the sink with all the venom I can muster, rinse, and then stare at my teeth, which are crooked; Danny's are straight. Dad and Mom say they can't afford to send me to a dentist. I try not to cry, but not even Buster's devotion to me as he sits at my feet takes away the dread of facing the kids at school again today, and every day.

Mom's gone, cussing at me as she left, telling me I take too long and she can't wait any longer...good! Danny's gone with her. His friends don't seem to notice the age of our car and I think they're too busy trying to keep in with him to tease him about it. Why don't parents realize that what they do or don't do makes it so hard for us kids at school, where the richest, prettiest, handsomest, fittest and most popular kids rule, leaving the rest of us to suffer the humiliation of being left out at best, and at worst, bullied for being a nerd.

Being an ugly nerd is the worst thing in the world. I brush my hair and clip it back behind my ears. I've asked Mom if she'll let me have it styled but she says I'm too young. I'm fourteen; all the girls in my class have their hair styled, why can't I. Money I guess. She gets her dressmaking scissors and hacks my hair off in a line around my neck, which looks as if she's put a bowl on my head and trimmed around it. I'm sick of it. When I grow up I'm going to get a good job that pays lots, and then I'll be able to have my hair styled the way I want it.

I kiss Buster goodbye and walk the four blocks to school. No one walks with me, even though I see some girls who are in the same classes I take; they ignore me as they walk past and I try to pretend that it doesn't matter to me, but it does.

A gang of boys pushes past me and one laughs in my face. "Parrot nose," he sneers, and his friends laugh. I put my head down and follow them without looking where I'm going; I just follow their jeering up the steps and into the building, and although I know there are many more kids that will poke fun of me in there, it feels a little safer because at least some grown-ups are around.

I take my place in the front of the class, knowing that I'm excluded from the back rows of desks where the popular kids are. It's an unwritten rule; Dad tells me that he and his friends all sat in the back row and the nerds sat in the front, with the "wannabe" kids in the middle. Although Danny's the same age as me, he's in another class, and every night he tells me about what he and the other kids get up to in the back row; he makes me sick. Can't he just shut up about it for one moment?

The problem with sitting in the front row with the nerds is that none of the nerds wants to be associated with you in case you're more nerdy than they are. It's a lonely place and is made worse by the constant snickering, which you just know is about you and not about the nerd you're sitting next to.

I have bruises on my body from the other nerds and the wannabe boys who all push past me when the bell goes for the next class as we hurry through the door and down the corridor to get to the next classroom. The back row boys don't seem to bruise me and I guess that's because I don't exist, for they're too busy making out with the pretty girls with straight teeth, long hair and perfect noses.

As we pile into the next classroom the same unwritten rule tells us where to sit, and this time I'm next to a guy with long, black, curly hair and spots that are about to explode nasty yellow pus all over his paper. I know the look on my face is telling him that I think he's more nerdy than I am, yet I don't seem able to stop myself from feeling disgusted.

My pencil drops to the floor and rolls under his desk. He picks it up and hands it to me without saying anything but there's something in his eyes, which aren't as piggy as mine, in fact they're a brilliant, vibrant blue. It's something that says, "I'm here on the nerdy front row too, and I know what it feels like; yes, I've got spots but I've got nice eyes if only someone would bother to look." I take the pencil and look at him; one of his front teeth is black. One of his spots is oozing. I'm grossed out, and I can't help it showing on my face.

"Pay attention!" the teacher shouts and I look forward, snapped out of my thoughts.

"Today we have a guest speaker, Miss Tina, who works with teenagers, and she's going to be teaching a class and starting a group during lunch break that any of you can go to if you want to."

A lady stands in front of us and I wonder if the back row is going to start the "game" they play when we have new speakers in class. I remember the day when a pastor came in to tell us about the work he did in his church, but he left half way through the lesson as the back row and the wannabes—and there was even one or two nerds that joined in—jeered and ridiculed him. I'd been embarrassed and had wanted to stand up and tell them all to shut up, but I couldn't because I knew that they'd rip me to pieces if I had, so I sat there feeling the man's pain, and my own shame.

Miss Tina stands in front of us and I wait, not scared, but weary. She looks like a nice lady and my anger is simmering, anticipating their game of "let's run you off," but I know that I won't be able to do anything about it if they start because I don't want to draw attention to myself.

"Hi, my name's Miss Tina and I work at Beach Haven. I don't know whether you know where it is, or what it is. I'm here to tell you that it's a place where we work to help teenagers be the best they can be, to grow into the finest people they're able to be, and to learn how to respect themselves and others. It's a place where teenagers recover from the traumatic things that have happened to them—they rest and grow. It's on the coast and is built right by the beach. How many of you have spent time on the beach?"

I dare to turn around. Turning around is not allowed by nerds, it's an unwritten rule, but I do it anyway and turn back quickly when Tessa flicks her blond hair over her shoulders and sticks her tongue out at me. There aren't very many hands up. It's fifty miles to the nearest beach; Mom and Dad tell us that the car won't make it and so I've never been.

Miss Tina asks everyone in turn why they haven't been to the beach and the kids say that their parents are too busy, it's dirty, full of sewage, food is too expensive, it's too crowded and they can't stand sand getting in the carpet at home.

She looks sad.

"Well, you know, I grew up on an island so there were beaches everywhere. I've been on quiet beaches, busy beaches, dirty beaches and those that just take you to a place where you forget that life can be tough."

She has my attention; my life *is* tough. I want to go to a place where it isn't tough and if sand gets in my carpet I don't care.

"Do you know that on a beach you can find all manner of life, all striving to stay alive despite it being really hard, for at any moment some creature is likely to eat you up. Sounds tough, doesn't it? And I wonder if that's how it feels for some of you, too."

The class has become quiet; straight teeth and long hair don't seem to matter anymore.

"I remember being taken to the beach as a child, and my sister and brothers would climb among the rocks when the tide was out. It was only then that the rocks were visible, for when the tide was in there was no beach and no rocks, they were all under water, but at low tide there was a whole new world waiting to be seen...with all its secrets."

❧ I rest my elbows on my desk and lean my head in my hands, listening to her.

"I wonder about that. Imagine standing on the cliff above a beach when the tide is in. You can only see what's on the surface, as beautiful as it is, but what about what's underneath the waves, what about what's *really* there? You know that just because the tide's in and you can't see all the life beneath the waves, it doesn't mean that it doesn't exist. You just have to hang around long enough to wait for the tide to go out, for the water to recede, to see another beauty, one that's hidden beneath the high tide."

I can hear some of the kids fidgeting and whispering.

"Do you have something to say?" she asks, and they're silenced; I feel a grin spread across my face.

"Looking at people is a bit like looking at a beach; they look one way at first glance but if you wait a while you'll see what's really underneath. Sometimes the surface can be rough and full of turbulence, like a stormy sea, and you'd never know that what lies beneath is beautiful and captivating.

"What I'd like you all to do is to write a sentence about what you think people see when they first see you, and another sentence to describe what's under the surface."

"Do we have to?" Tessa says, "This is stupid."

This is how they behaved when the pastor came to talk to us; she's starting to try and run Miss Tina off, but it doesn't happen because she answers in a way that stops Tessa from saying anything else.

"Are you finding it difficult to describe how others would see you, my dear? Or is it that you don't know what lies beneath the surface?"

Tessa sighs loudly but starts to write and no one else says anything.

My stomach has turned over and my hands are sweating with the thought of having to find something to write, something that I can read aloud in class that won't humiliate me.

"If you can't think of a sentence, a word will do, just a word, and don't worry—we're not going to be reading them aloud in class. So you can be honest and say what you really think, because only you and I will see what you've written."

That feels better, well, it does until I think about what to write that's honest. Others see me as an ugly nerd and what's beneath my ugly, nerdy surface is pain, terrible pain. I can't write that. I don't want myself to see it—let alone anyone else, even if she does seems a nice lady—yet it *is* what I write because it's the truth.

She tells us to put our names on the top of the paper and fold it into quarters, and then she walks around the class with a bowl, and we each drop our paper into it.

"Thank you for doing that," she says. "The whole purpose of that exercise is to help you to be aware that every human being presents himself to the world with a kind of mask on—a social persona, a social mask, how they want others to see them."

"How stupid," I think; I don't want others to *see* me as ugly, I just am ugly. I'd give anything to have a different face.

"No matter what kind of social mask you have it is sure to hide what's underneath, what is the *real* you. You know, sometimes we can get so hung up on what we look like, or what other people think of us, that we forget what's really inside us. And while we're so concerned with what we present to the world, our social selves, other people are trying to work out who we are, and the main clue they have to make assumptions about us is our social mask."

Everyone's quiet.

"Look at me. Write down what you think I like doing in my spare time."

I write the word, "sewing."

"Okay, shout out what you think it is."

"Flower arranging."

"Knitting."

"Crocheting."

"Cooking."

"Babysitting."

"Sewing," I say.

"Singing in church."

"Gardening."

"Swimming."

"Walking."

"Playing cards."

She's laughing as everyone shouts out and shaking her head. She holds up her hands to silence us, and grins.

"You're all wrong. I like riding Harley Davidson motorcycles."

I can hear some kids gasp and I turn around to see some of the boys staring at her in awe.

"My dad's got a Harley Davidson; it's cool."

"Can you see that you all made assumptions about

me just by looking at me, by my age, the clothes I'm wearing, my hair, and the fact that I'm a grown-up coming to teach one of your classes. Making assumptions like that is called stereotyping. Don't feel bad, we all do it, but it's only when we look deeper that we find out what someone is really like.

"Now, making assumptions like that is normally pretty harmless but sometimes it can be damaging to our self-esteem. What happens if someone has a birth mark on their face or a feature that makes them feel self conscious?"

My face is so red and hot that I feel faint. The class is silent. She pulls her chair from behind her table and sits among us.

"I want to tell you something. When I was a little girl I had to wear glasses and everyone called me "four eyes." It hurt my feelings, but something worse happened while I was a teenager, when it mattered a lot to me about whether the other kids liked me or not. I developed a really big mole on my top lip."

We're really quiet.

"It sat there on my lip getting bigger and bigger and my mother said that it had roots growing all over my face under the skin, so I knew that I could never get rid of it. I grew up knowing that no one would ever want to kiss me, and that no matter how hard I tried to make my social mask look nice, that ugly old mole sat there making people stare at me, and I could see disgust on their faces.

"Now, if someone had asked me to write down what people thought when they first saw me and a word to describe what was under my surface, I'd have written that they would have seen me as 'ugly' and what was beneath my surface was 'pain.'"

My face is so red that it's burning and I want to cry. This lady knows how I'm feeling; those are the two words I wrote.

"What happened to it?" the guy sitting next to me asks.

"I lived with it until I was grown-up and went to nursing school, and then one day while I was in the operating room, a kind surgeon cut it out for me. You know, I cried a lot, for had I known that it didn't have roots all over my face, I'd have had it removed years ago." She looks sad. "You know, people can be cruel. They stereotype, and they can be mean if they think you're different, and it can be just a small difference, nothing big, just a silly mole."

She starts to giggle. "You should have seen me. With my stitches in a row above my top lip I looked just like Adolph Hitler. Would you like to see the scar?"

She walks around the room and peers into everyone's face showing us a tiny scar that's barely noticeable to show us that her story is true and not made up. Finally she sits back down.

"D'you know what hurt me the most? Nobody except my family bothered to look beneath my surface to see what was there. They stopped only at the mole on my face. I can remember going out for dinner, and a man who I'd known for years came up to me and told me how beautiful I was and what a difference the surgery had made. I was *so* mad. I said, 'I'm the same as I always was,' but he didn't get it; he didn't know how to see anything beyond the social mask we all wear, or beyond the way a person looks."

The bell breaks into our thoughts, for the whole class is quiet, and suddenly we grab our books and head for the door. I look at Miss Tina as I leave and she smiles at me as if she can see something good beneath my surface, my hooked nose, crooked teeth and sunken, piggy eyes; and I hope she can, because I can't. All I feel is pain.

"See you all next week. Be safe and kind to each other," she calls behind us.

Her voice stays with me all day but it obviously doesn't with the other kids because they're as mean as ever, bumping into me in the cafeteria, making me drop my lunch, then spilling water into my lap when I finally sit down to eat a bag of chips. I want to cry but don't. I harden my face to show that they haven't hurt me and think about the "mask" Miss Tina says we all wear. Why does mine have to be like this, wounded and sullen, when I look around and see the other girls with "masks" that smile and flirt with the boys? They're enjoying themselves. My life's a misery from the moment I wake up to the moment I go to sleep; if only God had given me a pretty face, then I'd be able to wear the same "mask" as the pretty girls and have all the boys want me, too. I leave the cafeteria, wet, hungry and humiliated.

The afternoon's no better and I walk home trying my best to ignore the comments the kids shout out as I pass with my head down.

I let myself in and the house is silent. Danny must be at baseball practice and Mom must have taken Buster for a walk because he's not here. That's odd. She never takes him for a walk. I wander about the house feeling depressed.

It's ages before Danny comes home.

"Where's Mom?" he asks.

"I don't know. Buster's not here either. Perhaps she's taking him for a walk."

Danny looks at me as if I'm stupid, and says, "Yeah, really."

He microwaves some pasta that's left over in the fridge and flops in front of the TV.

The car pulls up in the drive and I stand up to look out of the window. It's Dad.

He opens the door and immediately I can see something's wrong in his face even before he blurts it out.

"Your mother's left us, gone off with another man. She can't expect me to manage this house, you two and a dog all by myself, so I had no choice but to put the dog down."

I can't think straight; my head's spinning so badly that it takes a few seconds for what he's just said to sink in. Did he just say that he's killed my dog?

"Where's Buster?" I demand.

"I've just told you. Your mother's run off with another man and I can't cope with you two and a dog, so the dog had to go. It's her fault; don't blame me. It's not my fault."

I scream so loudly that it feels as if it's coming from the television and not from me. I'm only vaguely aware that Danny is staring at me with a look that I hardly ever see in his face—concern—as Dad slaps me hard across the face.

"Stop it!" he shouts at me. "It's only a God-damned dog. You should be crying about your mother leaving us, not over a stupid dog."

My screaming is now not only shock and grief but anger too, and I wish that he'd been "put down," along with my mother as well. He slaps me again and this time I try to hit him back, over and over, until he slaps me so hard that I fall to the floor, then he walks out of the door.

"I hate him," I sob, and Danny doesn't know what to do as I haul myself up with my face stinging badly and I run out of the door, not to stop Dad from driving off—I'll never speak to him again—but to get away from the house; the house that's empty now without my precious dog.

Danny doesn't try to stop me.

I don't know where I'm going, I just walk and walk, my eyes blinded with tears. People are calling at me from their cars and I ignore them as I cry. After awhile I get short of breath from trying to walk and cry at the same time.

An older boy I've seen at school starts walking with me and I ignore him but he keeps asking me, "What's the matter?" And since I've got a pain in my side from walking so fast, I stop.

"You look like you're in trouble, girl," he says. "Smoke?"

I shake my head. No, I don't smoke. I can't even afford to buy another school dinner when some kid makes me drop mine.

"Here, you look like you could do with some help; smoke this."

He pushes a squashed cigarette into my mouth that smells funny, and because I hate everyone so bad, particularly my mom and dad, I do as he says and suck on the end of it. It chokes me, but he tells me to do it again and it'll be easier. It isn't, but I do it anyhow and cough until I can't cough anymore.

I don't feel as if I'm here anymore, and suddenly I don't feel so desperate.

"C'mon baby, come with me," he says.

No one has called me "baby" before. I'm an ugly nerd, the one with the other nerds in the front row of class.

He slips his hand behind my head and kisses me;

a long, slow, lingering kiss that makes me forget all about my mom running off, my dad killing my dog, and every kid in school hating me because I'm ugly.

I don't know what's happening to me because I can't feel my feet, and I have no idea which way is up or which way is down. I'm giggling like someone has just told me something really funny but I can't remember what it is. He takes my hand, and the only thing I can remember is that he's pulling my arm and I'm following, tripping over and giggling. He says he's going to take me home. I think I may have said that I don't want to go home, but he says that he's going to take me no matter what.

He pulls me across the road and I lean against his car while he unlocks the door. I fall into the seat, giggling, and have no idea where he's driving to. He stops the car and lights up another cigarette and pushes it into my mouth. I think I might be sick, and somewhere deep inside of me I'm glad that I haven't eaten all day, because to vomit after eating feels really bad—it's so messy. So as I suck on the cigarette I don't care if I'm sick, I've got nothing to lose.

My head's spinning, my stomach's warm and I'm giggling; everything that hurts is just beyond my grasp. I don't know how it happens, but he pushes me down on the back seat of his car and he's on top of me. He's saying I'm beautiful as he pulls at my clothes. No one's ever said I'm beautiful before, no one, not my mom or my dad, no one. He tells me I'm beautiful over and over, and it feels good. For the first time in my life I feel that someone wants me and that I'm special, so I don't stop him from touching me.

My head is spinning round and round so much that it doesn't hurt; I'm barely aware of what he's doing and it's over really quickly. When I say that I think I'm going to throw up, he opens the door and pulls me out.

"Don't throw up in the car; it's my dad's, and he'll go crazy." He stands next to me but doesn't kiss me anymore. Perhaps he thinks I'm going to chuck up over him.

"We'd better get going," he says, and rolls the window down telling me again not to throw up in the car. I don't remember telling him where I live but he drops me at the end of the road and I stagger up to the front door and hammer on it, having forgotten my key.

The door opens.

"Where have you been? I've been worried out of my mind," says my mom.

I start crying. What's she doing here? Dad said that she'd gone...he killed my dog because she'd gone.

My head is floating somewhere else but I manage to blurt out, "Dad said you'd run off with another man and that you weren't coming back."

I'm feeling so sick that I want to vomit. There's

a funny feeling between my legs. It's wet and a bit sore, and I want to have a shower.

"Dad killed my dog because you'd gone," I cry, and Mom wrings her hands not knowing what to say. There isn't anything *to* say, is there? Nothing can bring him back.

"I'll get you a new one," she pleads, but I storm off to the bathroom.

"I don't want a *new* one, I just want Buster." How can she think that she can just buy a new one and it'll be all right? He's not a ripped pair of jeans that can be replaced.

As I stand under the jets of water I cry, not caring if she can hear me or not. I stand under the shower for as long as it takes for the water to run cold and my body to stop smarting. I shiver in the chilling water thinking about what my dad's done, what my mom's done, and what I've done, all in one day.

I go to bed weighed down with thoughts. My bed is the cold place it always is, and it seems colder knowing that there'll be no warm furry Buster to share it with in the morning, he who gives me unconditional love. I don't have to be pretty or smart, Buster loves me no matter what, but now he's gone.

Too much has happened today; the day seems too full and too fast. There was me not taking a shower, school with all its bullying, a new lady, Miss Tina, who seemed to know exactly what I was feeling, Dad killing the only friend I have after nothing more than a fight with Mom, which happens all the time, and then a nameless boy doing the "thing" to me. It's the thing that all the girls in the back row in class talk about all the time, which I never thought I'd ever be a part of, being an ugly, hooked nose nerd on the first row at school. Maybe now I'll have something in common with them, something I can reach them with, if only they'll listen. I can be one of them.

Someone wanted me that way tonight. That means I must be okay.

Chapter Two

I don't sleep very well. I'm sore, but my heart hurts more than my body does, and in the morning when there's no Buster to lick my face, there's an ache in my heart that refuses to go away.

Mom nags me to hurry again and I deliberately take my time. I'm so angry with her and Dad; if they hadn't argued my dog would still be here. She leaves the house without me and I trudge my way to school.

There's a flicker of excitement in my stomach though, despite the ache in my heart, and I wonder if the boy will be there or if I'll get to see him. I ignore all the kids who call me "beaky" and "parrot nose" as I walk up the school steps and go through the main doors. He had said that I was beautiful and I'm going to keep that thought in my head so that the others can't hurt me.

All day I look for him and try to ignore everyone as they push me about, knocking my books out of my hands and calling me names. Finding him becomes my lifeline, and it isn't until lunch recess that I spot him with a crowd of boys hanging around over in the far corner of the baseball field. I want to go over to him but I'm a bit nervous, so I sit on a bench and hope that he'll notice me.

He does. He and the other boys come over towards me and my heart starts racing, but they walk by laughing together. I feel crushed and want to cry. He told me I was beautiful; perhaps he's just shy in front of his friends—yes, that's what it is.

I go to my last class, unable to ignore the taunts anymore, and I don't hear anything the teacher says, as my ears seem only to pick up the whispers behind me.

I'm so relieved when the bell rings and I can get out of here, but I hang back for a while to let everyone go first; I've learned that it's safer that way. There are kids in the halls arm in arm, good-looking kids, popular kids, not like me.

I get outside and most of the kids have gone. As I walk through the gates a boy walks up to me...he's one of those with the boy I was with last night. I'm sure this boy is one of his friends. I look away but he starts talking to me.

"Hey, I'm Jeff. Hold up, wait." He grabs me by the arm and looks at me, saying, "Did anyone ever tell you that you've got pretty eyes?"

I thought he was going to say something to hurt me, but as I hear his words I smile at him and feel shy.

"You wanna go out with me?" he asks, and before I can answer he says, "Meet me in the park at six." Then he turns around and runs down the road.

My heart suddenly feels light again. I can't be that bad if someone wants to go out with me, can I?

I barely get my key in the door before I hear Mom and Dad screaming at each other again. Mom's crying and throwing things while Dad is telling her to get out. I try to shout, "Stop it," but my voice gets drowned out by their screaming, so I walk past them and go to my room.

I lie on my bed and think about Jeff. Shall I go? Mom and Dad wouldn't let me if they knew, that's for sure. I want a boyfriend so badly. Everyone who's pretty has a boyfriend; perhaps people will leave me alone if I've got a boyfriend.

I can hear Mom screaming even louder and suddenly the door slams and it's quieter. There's only Dad talking to himself, calling her all sorts of nasty things, almost as nasty as the things I get called at school. When he sounds calmer I venture out of my room. He's in the bathroom shaving.

"Your mother's gone for good. That's the end of it. She's no good; there's plenty more where she came from."

He gets dressed up; he never bothers to get dressed up.

"Where're you going?" I ask.

"Not that it's any of your business but I'm going out. If she can find somebody else so can I. Get your own dinner." Then he's gone.

I sit around for a while with the TV on to fill the silence, but I don't pay it any attention. Has my mom really gone? She didn't even say goodbye. I don't exist to my mom and dad. They don't care about me at all. I don't think they really care about Danny either, but he doesn't seem to be bothered. I sit here feeling so alone and confused that when I see it's nearly six o'clock I jump up and head for the park. If they don't care about me, then I'll let someone else care about me.

Jeff's waiting by the gates.

"I didn't know if you'd show up," he says. "I don't have a car, and my dad won't let me borrow his yet, but I'll have one soon. Let's go in here."

I follow him into the park and there's no one here. There're ducks waddling about, but no people. We sit on a park bench and he puts his arm around me. I don't stop him, even though I don't know him and have only just met him, for it feels nice to have someone, anyone, be nice to me. No one's ever nice to me so I'm not going to push him away. He kisses me and I can hear him breathing fast as his hands start to move all over my body. He tells me I'm pretty and I've got a beautiful body and that he wants to go out with me for ever and ever. It feels so wonderful to hear him whispering all these things hotly into my ear that for one small moment I don't feel alone anymore; I don't feel ugly or bullied. Someone wants me. It doesn't occur to me to stop him, for if this is the price I have to pay to feel this way, then I'll do it with him. If I say "No," he'll walk away and then I won't have anyone.

He's quick and I'm back indoors before six thirty. I don't feel quite right and I'm not sure why.

I shower and try to find something to eat in the fridge but there's nothing worth eating, so I don't bother. I sit on the couch curled up, hugging my knees. I've got a boyfriend. He said he wanted to go out with me forever; perhaps now it'll start to get better for me at school.

There's nothing to do so I go to bed and I'm awakened in the middle of the night by someone giggling. I creep to my door and pull it ajar. My dad's taking a woman dressed in a very short skirt into his and Mom's room. I don't know what to do. I want to leave my room and tell him that he can't take another woman into his and Mom's bed, but I know he'll be mad at me, so I don't. I lie in bed and feel revolted, hearing him grunting and groaning with her squealing and shouting "Yes" over and over. It's disgusting. I try to deaden the noise by clamping my pillow over my head but then I can't breathe, so I just have to endure it until it stops.

She's gone by the morning and so is Dad. The house feels empty as Danny slept over with his friend last night. I guess having me in the house didn't matter to Dad.

I go to school knowing that I don't matter at home and neither at school, but I do matter to Jeff. Finding him's easy—he and his mates are on the baseball field again and this time I don't feel as nervous as I did yesterday. He said we were going out together and would be forever. I hope he kisses me in front of his friends; that'll show everyone that I've got a boyfriend.

They all turn around when I walk up to them, but Jeff isn't smiling at me, he's laughing; they all are.

"Hey, slut, can I have a go?" three other boys jeer, as Jeff and the boy I first met laugh so hard that they hold each other up.

"C'mon, give us a bit, we'll even pay you, if you like. I've got a dime, c'mon."

I'm so stunned as they walk towards me unzipping their pants that I can't move. My feet seem to have stuck to the ground. One of them has actually got his thingy out and is waving it at me.

"God, how did you manage it, Jeff? She's so ugly. Did you put a bag over her head, or what?"

I don't hear anything else because suddenly I can move, so I turn and run as fast as I can, tears pouring down my face as their laughter still rings in my ears. There are groups of pretty girls all laughing at me as I run past them. Couples stop kissing each other and laugh. They must know what I did, because they shout "Slut" as I run away.

I don't bother to pick up my bag or jacket but just run out of the school gates to the only place I can go...home, but there's no comfort for me there either. No one wants me, no one, not my mom, my dad, my brother, no one at school and certainly no boy wants me. I feel dirty and used, and worse than I've ever felt in my life.

No one's home. I'm sobbing so loudly that it echoes through the empty house. I long for Buster but he's not here either. As I sob I start to wretch and run to the bathroom, but there's nothing in my stomach to bring up. I catch sight of my face in the mirror. This is what's wrong...my face. If only I was pretty everyone would like me and I'd be happy and popular. I gasp for breath as I hold on to the sink, staring at myself, seeming to see deep into my sunken piggy eyes to a place beyond this bathroom, beyond this pain, to a place where there is no pain, where there's nothing. And suddenly I know what I have to do.

I tip our four toothbrushes out of the mug and fill it with water, and then I open the cabinet and pour all the pills from every bottle into my hand. With one last look at my ugly face I say goodbye, and I'm glad; I hate me. Then I swallow mouthful after mouthful of pills and wash them down with the water, which tastes of the dregs of toothpaste and spit.

I lie on my bed and I miss my dog more than ever. I'm going to die and I wish he was here, but as the emptiness numbs me, a thread of thought cheers me up...I'm going to be with him soon.

I feel strangely calm and even my crying has stopped. There's a part of me that feels spiteful as I lie here waiting to leave this earth. I hope those boys will feel guilty for ever and ever, and I hope my mom feels guilty for leaving me and for giving me the worst face a girl could have, and I hope my dad feels guilty for killing my dog. I hope Danny feels guilty for doing nothing to help me. I hope all the kids at school will feel guilty too, for the way they've bullied me every single day and made my life a living hell. I can't help being a nerd. I blame my mom for that and I also blame God. Why couldn't I look more like Danny and take after Dad?

My thoughts, mingled with so much despair and pain, become slower and slower in my head until they stop...

• • • •

I can't find Buster. If this is heaven, it feels like hell. Where's Buster? I hear a voice shouting in my ear and suddenly something huge is forced down my throat, and from somewhere far away I'm aware that I'm gagging. Tears spring from my eyes when I see that I'm lying on a table and nurses are all around me with buckets, pipes, funnels and water, lots of it.

"If you *will* do this to yourself," a nurse says nastily, "then don't be surprised if it hurts to put you right. You need your ass spanked, putting your parents through all this."

I gag and gag as they pour water down through the tube to wash my stomach out. It's yanked here and there, and they are rough as they pull the tube down towards the bucket on the floor then up again to pour more water down into my stomach. My throat is raw, and although I can't talk, I know I'm crying because my face is wet, and it's not only from the splashes as the nurse pours more water into the funnel above my head.

Even as my whole world is falling apart, she lets me know how much contempt she has for people who waste her time, who aren't really ill and who should be thankful that they're healthy. Eventually she pulls the tube out from my stomach really roughly and I continue to gag even after she's left the room.

I didn't think I could feel worse than when I ran away from those boys, but I was wrong, this feels ten times worse. I wanted to be dead. I wanted my life to be over so that I wouldn't have to endure any more pain. But here I am, still here and things are worse—I've got a horrid nurse reminding me how awful I am. I rest back into the pillow, and tears fall silently down my face while I'm consumed with misery.

I can hear Dad outside, and Danny. They come in

a moment later and I can see that Dad's mad.

"You can thank your brother for saving your life. If he hadn't come home when he did, you'd be dead."

Oh, so it's Danny I have to thank for my misery, is it?

"I wish he hadn't come home," is all I can think of to say, and Dad is even more mad. Danny just stands there with something on his face that looks like fear and sorrow, I don't know. I don't *know* Danny, so I may be wrong. He suddenly looks very young and I wonder if I look as young to him.

"The doctor says you have to go somewhere; you can't come home."

I don't care; I don't want to go home. My mom's gone, and dad's killed Buster, so why would I want to go home? And I'm never going back to that school again, never. They can do what they like to me, I don't care, but I'm never going back there again.

I turn my face away from Dad and he walks out of the room, cussing about me. Danny stands by the side of my bed and puts his hand on my arm, and says, "I hate what he did to Buster. It wasn't fair." Then he walks away too as I stare at the wall and don't answer him. He's never helped me at school. He's popular, he's good looking, he's with the "in-crowd," and he's never once told anyone to leave me alone or helped me when he could see the kids being hateful towards me. I don't want to hear what he has to say about Buster. He's never cared about him, never loved him like I did, never needed him either, like I did, so I don't want to hear what he thinks now.

He leaves too and I'm alone. I'm glad. Only I'm not alone, for there's a mirror in the room and I can see myself lying on the bed, my hair full of vomit, my sunken piggy eyes red raw from crying, my hooked nose is running and my crooked teeth taste of vomit. I'm not alone, I'm still with me, and the way I feel right now, it feels unbearable. I know that whatever happens I'm going to get rid of my life and do a better job of it next time. No one will miss me, no one. What's the point of me being here if this is all there is to my life—suffering; everyone who knows me rejects me and even those who don't know me reject me, so what's the point?

I fall asleep and am awakened by two paramedics who tell me that they're taking me to a place where I'll be looked after. I don't want to be looked after; I just want to die. Why can't they all leave me alone and go and save someone who wants to be saved? But they ignore my sullen face and try to make me laugh by telling jokes. There's no laughter in me, in fact, there's nothing in me, nothing, so their jokes roll over my head, and I feel as if I'm not here, as if I don't exist.

They wheel me out to the ambulance in a wheel chair and I ignore the nurse who snaps at me saying,

"And don't you be doing this again, young lady." I so want to say something vile but I just haven't got the energy. I don't have any energy for hatred or for love, neither life nor death.

The two men strap me into the back of the ambulance and one stays with me while the other drives, and they continue trying to make me talk. Somewhere inside me I recognize that they care about what they do, but my despair is so bad that I'm just too far gone for them to help me with jokes, or by trying to get me to talk. Nothing matters to me so I don't want to answer their questions about school, home, hobbies, or anything; none of it matters to me at all.

I sit in silence and they finally give up, and I'm grateful for the silence. It seems ages until they pull up in front of a building that has a huge sign with "Beach Haven, a place to rest and grow," written on it. Somewhere in my numbed brain I know that I've heard of it before but I can't place where, nor do I care. The paramedics wheel me through the front door and one of them rubs my shoulder and says, "You'll be all right here, don't you worry."

They wheel me down a corridor and a door opens. A lady smiles at me and suddenly I know why I've heard of this place. It's the lady that came to our school a few days ago—Miss Tina, the lady who knew my feelings without even talking to me. I want to cry, and do. Something inside me lets go when I see her because her answers to the questions she gave us were the same as mine. She knows what it's like to be ugly and she knows what it's like to feel pain.

She kneels down in front of me and gives me a hug and I let her. As the two paramedics leave I hear them say that my mom's left and Dad refused to come with us, "Couldn't be bothered, if you ask me."

That sounds like Dad. Too much trouble, kids are, a bit like dogs really, and I'm surprised that he didn't have me put down along with Buster.

Miss Tina talks to me and asks me all kinds of questions, and when we get to the bit about school her face lights up.

"I went there to teach a few days ago."

"I know, I was in your class."

Miss Tina says, "You know, I've been thinking about you because, when I got home and looked at all the answers the class gave me to the two questions I asked, yours were the same as mine. Do you know that?"

I nod.

"Ugly and pain." I frown. "But Miss Tina, you're not ugly."

"Ah, but I thought I was, that's the difference. We may not be ugly, but if we think we are, then that's how it feels to us. You're not ugly, Melody, you're beautiful," she tells me, and immediately I shut her out. It's not true. I *am* ugly, and after Jeff and his friend lied to me saying I was beautiful, I'll never believe anyone who says it again. They wanted to make a fool of me. I know what I am...I'm ugly and a nerd.

I turn away from her, ignoring everything she asks me and refuse to answer. She takes me up a massive staircase and along a corridor to my room, pats my back, and I ignore her when she says, "Sleep tight. We'll work together to make it all come right. Try not to worry, sweet girl. You'll be okay. We're here to help you. God bless." Then she's gone.

I lie in my bed hating that I'm still alive but glad to be away from Dad and school. I don't know what I think about Danny; okay, he hasn't helped me like he could have, but he looked pretty worried at the hospital. Perhaps we've both been so busy trying to cope with Mom and Dad's arguments that we haven't had time to connect with each other. I don't know, and I'm too tired to work any of it out.

• • • •

When I wake up *things* feel different, but *I* don't feel different; I still wish I weren't alive, but things feel different around me. There are kids my own age here and some of them I know would be in the front row at school along with me, but not all of them—some are pretty.

As we eat breakfast in the dining room the other kids ask me why I'm here; I feel shy and don't want to say.

"I'm here because I tried to kill my stepfather after he tried to have sex with me," one girl says.

"I'm here because I'm depressed...I found my mom hanging in her bedroom."

They shock me, and suddenly it becomes okay to say why I'm here.

"I'm here because I tried to kill myself," I say. I don't feel ashamed; they make it okay to say how it is. They don't seem surprised and dig into their eggs and pancakes, so I do, too.

"It's good here," a girl called Freddie says. "They really try to help you." Perhaps she can see that I'm anxious because she says, "You'll be okay."

We have to do all kinds of things here, like chores, which some kids moan about but which seem really easy to me. I guess it depends on how much you're used to doing at home, and I'm used to doing everything, so this is like a holiday to me. We're allowed to walk along the beach and it's very beautiful, and I guess that's why it's called Beach Haven. I remember Miss Tina telling us when she came to our school about how things look on the surface but when the tide's out you can see what's really there. Now that I can actually see the sea and breathe the smell of the seaweed lying along the shoreline, I can really understand what she was trying to tell us in class. Sometimes the shore looks one way and another time it looks another way, yet it's still the same underneath.

We have to go to group here and that's really hard

at times because we have to talk about why we're here. It means admitting to everyone that I'm ugly and a nerd, and I'm scared of what they'll say.

Freddie sits next to me while we're sitting on the beach.

"I'll do your hair for you later if you want. Will you do mine? I like it braided?"

I'm embarrassed. I don't know how to do hair. My mom's never shown me so I don't know what to say.

She looks at me and my silence upsets her. She gets up and walks off, and I'm left alone. I want to cry. I've never had a friend before and I don't know how to be one.

It's time to go back in so I follow the others back inside, praying that Freddie will talk to me, but she doesn't.

I go to my room and cry, my loneliness as acute as it was the first day I came here. Miss Tina is in the doorway.

"What's the matter, sweet girl? Why are you crying?"

"Freddie doesn't like me anymore," and I feel stupid and a cry-baby for saying it.

"It's time for group, perhaps you can work it out then. C'mon, it'll be all right."

I follow her downstairs and go into the Group Room, which has lots of chairs in a circle. I always feel scared in this room because anyone can say anything, and I've never known a place where honesty can sit next to respect and still be friends.

I look at the floor feeling sick.

I'm barely listening as the other kids start talking about their feelings and why they're at Beach Haven, because all I can think of is Freddie. I look at her and she's looking at me.

She suddenly speaks out. "We're told that we should say what we're feeling and thinking, and by saying it out loud it keeps communication open and honest."

"That's right," Miss Tina says. "What is it that you want to say, Freddie?"

She takes a deep breath and I feel sick.

"Well, I feel hurt because when I offered to do Melody's hair and asked her if she'd do mine, she ignored me. I thought we were friends. I feel hurt."

I start to cry because I hate the fact that I've hurt the only friend I've ever had. She looks angry with me and all I did was to be silent, and I was only silent because I didn't know what to say.

Miss Tina says, "Would you like to answer, Melody? Remember, everyone's okay here, so it's okay to say what's on your mind."

I stutter and feel awful. "I'm sorry I hurt your feelings, Freddie. I've never had a friend before, and I don't know how to do hair. My mom never showed me. She wouldn't let me have my hair styled; it's like she put a bowl on my head and cut my hair off around it to get the shape right."

I start to cry, not only because I've offended my new friend, and I'm desperate for her to still like me, but because talking about how my mom never helped me hurts.

"So, are you saying that you didn't answer Freddie because you don't know how to do hair, and not because of any other reason?" Miss Tina asks.

"Yes," I say quickly. "I really like you, Freddie, and if someone will show me how to do hair, I'd love to do it for you, but I don't think you'll be able to do anything to mine; my mom's messed it up."

Miss Tina says, "Hair grows and whatever is messed up grows out."

I think about what she's just said and smile, wishing life was like that...perhaps it is.

"I'm sorry if I hurt you, Freddie," I say. "Will you show me how to do hair?"

"Of course I will," she says, smiling at me and suddenly I feel so much better.

It's hard having a friend. I've wanted one all my life, and now that I have one it's not so easy to get it right all the time. I have to learn how to be honest and say what I think, or what's going on for me inside, so that she doesn't misunderstand me.

Miss Tina looks at me.

"You say your mom always messed your hair up. Can you say more about that?"

"She said that she didn't have money to waste on taking me to have it styled so she did it herself, but she did it so poorly that everyone at school made fun of me. I'm already ugly but she made it worse. Sometimes I think she did it deliberately."

"Listen, Melody, let me tell you that you are not ugly. This is an issue for you to work on while you're here, to learn to like yourself. Can you say more about why you think that she may have messed your hair up deliberately?"

I don't want to. It all feels too deep, too scary.

"I don't know. I begged her to let me grow it long so that I could be the same as the other girls at school, but she wouldn't let me. She just hacked it off."

I'm crying. "She didn't even cut it properly, it was all jagged and uneven. The kids at school ripped me to pieces and I hated her for it. I'm already ugly but my hair made me look worse."

"I'm going to say this to you over and over, Melody, you are not ugly..."

I cut her short. "I'm not pretty, and if you tell me I am, I'll know you're lying."

She's quiet for a moment.

"Melody, have you heard of the saying, 'Beauty is in the eye of the beholder'?"

I shake my head.

"It means that what may seem beautiful to one person may not be to another, and what may seem ugly to one person may seem beautiful to another. We are all different and that's the way God meant us to be. You *are* beautiful."

I look away from her, not satisfied.

Freddie says, "Do you think your mom was jealous of you in some way?"

Miss Tina smiles at her and nods, saying, "Good question."

"I don't know. She's ugly and I look like her, so why would she be jealous of me?"

Another girl, who I think is called Tammy, says, "You're younger than her and got your whole life ahead of you. Maybe she's jealous of that."

Freddie asks, "Do you look *exactly* like your mom?"

"Almost, but I have my Dad's lips."

"And do you think they're pretty?" Miss Tina asks.

I nod reluctantly, not wanting to admit the fact that a part of me might be pretty, for it doesn't fit with how I see myself.

Chapter Three

As we leave the Group Room, Freddie sidles up beside me and says, "Let me do your hair and I'll show you how to do mine on someone else, then you'll be able to do it."

I smile at her. This is all new to me, to have a friend. I don't know how much is too much or too little. I don't know how to be close to someone and I'm scared to get too close in case they run away.

As we sit in the lounge she starts to separate my hair into sections and begins braiding. Tammy sits with us and watches, waiting for Freddie to show me how to do it on her.

"Y'know, my mom is jealous of me. She's fat and hates it that I'm thin. She's constantly trying to make me eat; we're always arguing about it. D'you think your mom *is* jealous of you?"

"I don't know. I'm as ugly as she is, so why would she be?"

Freddie pulls my hair and makes me yell.

"You're not ugly. Okay, your teeth are crooked, but you can fix that."

"How? My parents can't afford to take me to a dentist."

"Oh, I don't know. Maybe you'll have to wait until you're grown up, when you've got a job, and then you can pay for it yourself. But it's still fixable," she says.

"Yeah, but what about my eyes? They're sunken and piggy; that's not fixable."

Both of them pull a face and sigh loudly.

"Girl, haven't you heard of makeup?"

"Of course I have. My mom uses it all the time, but it doesn't make her look any better."

Tammy says, "Well, maybe she doesn't put it on right or doesn't know what suits her. You just have to learn how to do it so that it enhances your features."

"Enhances, eh? Big word," Freddie teases.

"You know what I mean," Tammy says, kicking out at her. "Making the best of what you've got, okay?"

"I'll do your makeup for you if you like," Freddie says.

"I don't have any." I feel embarrassed. "Mom wouldn't let me wear it and said that she couldn't afford to buy me any. She told me I was too young anyway, and said that she didn't care if all the girls at school were wearing it, I wasn't going to."

"You can borrow mine," she says, and I feel more grateful than I can say.

Freddie's sixteen and says that she's been wearing it since she was twelve.

"I'm lucky," she says. "My sister went to beauty college to be a beautician, so she showed me how to do it so that you don't end up looking like a clown. She always says, 'Less is more,' and I guess she means that using just a little in exactly the right places *enhances* (she pokes her tongue out at Tammy, who laughs) your natural beauty. That's what *she* says anyway."

I don't say anything because I don't think I've got any natural beauty and I don't know how she's going to enhance what's not there, but I don't want to appear ungrateful, so I stay quiet.

My hair is finished and I look in the mirror marvelling at how different it looks, although as far as I can see it does nothing to change my sunken piggy eyes and hooked nose.

She opens her makeup bag and tips all kinds of things onto the table.

"Right, here we go. Ready?"

I nod, feeling some trepidation. She talks at me all the time she's dabbing color onto my face, telling me what to do and what not to do. She stands back to take a good look when she's finished and smiles.

"Take a look," she says.

I don't look like me anymore. She's done something to my eyes that doesn't make them seem sunken or piggy anymore; in fact, they stand out so much that I barely notice my hooked nose.

Tammy says, "You look great."

I continue to stare at myself in the mirror, dumbfounded.

"You should be a makeup artist when you grow up," I say.

"That's what I hope to do if I can get my grades back up and keep myself out of trouble."

She starts to show me how to braid Tammy's hair so that I can do hers, and I watch really intently because I want to do it properly.

Tammy helps me and I do it. Freddie looks in the mirro,r and we try to hold one behind her head so that she can see all the way around.

"Thanks, you did a good job," she says.

After dinner we have to go to another group and I feel a bit anxious. Two of the boys say that I look nice, but I'm wary of them and look away.

Almost as soon as Miss Tina starts to talk, both the boys pounce on me and I feel attacked.

"I gave you a compliment and you completely ignored me," Paul says.

"Me too," says Rick. "If you've got no friends, maybe it's because you ignore them."

I feel hurt and angry. I long for friends at school, but no one wants to be friends with me. They think

I'm a nerd. If I ignore people it's because they hurt me by saying I'm ugly.

Miss Tina asks, "Is there some truth in that, Melody?"

I start crying again and I'm mad at myself for crying yet again, but it all feels so painful that I can't stop it. I feel as if they are blaming me for all the horrid things the kids at school do to me.

"I only ignore the kids at school because they call me names and laugh at me for being ugly."

Paul speaks out. "But I wasn't being nasty to you. I wasn't calling you names or laughing at you. I gave you a compliment, that's all."

Jeff and the boy, whose name I don't know, flash into my mind and I hear the hollow compliments they gave me echoing around my head and their laughter as they called me a slut. I am consumed with shame and hide my face behind my hands and sob.

"What is it?" Miss Tina asks. "You're quite safe here. What's upsetting you so much?"

It seems ages until I can get enough breath to talk and I'm so afraid, for if I tell them what I've done, they may all hate me and think that I *am* a slut.

Miss Tina stands up and walks over to me and kneels down on one knee, pulling my hands away from my face.

"Melody, this is a place where everybody is safe, everybody is respected and no one will judge you. You can say anything you like and it will be okay. Do you believe me?"

I nod my head. I have to because every kid in the group is looking at me with concern on their face; not one is laughing at me.

"Tell us what troubles you so much."

So between sobs I tell them that because two boys had given me compliments I had sex with them, thinking that they really did like me. I feel so humiliated as it spills out of me, and stupid, too. How could I have been that gullible or naïve?

A girl called Julie who looks really pretty starts to speak. "That happened to me, too."

"How?" I ask, "You're really pretty."

She shrugs, "If you say so; I don't see it. I was having a hard time when my parents were getting a divorce. They fought all the time, mainly about who was going to get custody of me, but while they were fighting over me it was like I didn't exist, and they weren't there for me at all. I felt so alone that when a boy at school started paying me lots of attention, I couldn't bear the thought of losing him and being alone again. He said that he'd find another girlfriend if I didn't have sex with him, and I couldn't bear to be without him, so I did it. But he left me anyway, so not only did I feel alone, I felt used and dirty as well. He told everyone at school, like he was proud of it or something. Then other boys thought I was easy and tried to get me to do it with them, too. It was awful."

"But you can get a boyfriend. You're pretty," I say.

Rick says, "I really like a girl in my class who my friends say isn't pretty, but I think she's fine. She makes me laugh and listens to me when I want to talk. I don't think I'd care at all about whether she's *pretty* or not. You're too stuck on people being pretty; that's what I think. I think I'd be scared to get to know you in case you thought I wasn't good looking enough, because all you seem to care about is looks."

I'm shocked at what he's saying.

Miss Tina says, "Y'know, looks don't really matter, it's who you are that counts, whether you're friendly, kind and considerate or fun to be with. And if someone only wants to go out with you because of how you look, then they're shallow and don't deserve to be in your company. Thanks, Rick.

"Going back to what Julie was saying, it doesn't matter what you look like, you can still feel vulnerable or lonely and it's times like that when you can make the wrong choice for the wrong reasons. Having sex with someone because they pressure you into it, or because you are scared that they'll leave you, is never the right reason for sleeping with someone, nor will it make someone like you more, or stay with you."

She turns toward me and says, "I know that being bullied must have made you feel very bad, but did something else happen that made you feel even more vulnerable and lonely?"

Buster pops into my head and I start to sob again, and it's a while before I can trust myself to talk. They all sit there and wait for me to stop.

"The night I first had sex, I had run away from the house because my dad had..." I can't seem to get it out, the pain crushes my chest and I'm having trouble breathing.

They're all staring at me, although I can barely see them through my tears.

"...Killed my dog."

Miss Tina frowned. "Did you just say that your dad had killed your dog?"

I nod, and some of the girls gasp while others cuss.

"But why, what happened?" she asks, still frowning.

Freddie hands me a box of tissues and I blow my nose noisily.

"He said that Mom had left with another man and that he couldn't cope with two kids and a dog as well, so he took him to the vet and had him put down."

A fresh wave of sobs comes over me and threatens to drown me.

Miss Tina is still wearing her frown.

"Whose dog was it? Was it your mother's?"

I shake my head. "It was my dog. I loved him. He was the only one who loved me in that house."

"Did you look after him?"

"Yes," I say, feeling confused, hurt and angry all at once. "I did everything for him. I fed him, I bathed him and I took him for walks. I even cleaned up his mess. They didn't do anything for him."

Rick says, "Then why did your dad say that he wouldn't be able to cope with the dog if he didn't do anything to help look after him?"

I shake my head. "I don't know."

"What happened when he told you this?" Miss Tina asks.

"I wanted to die. Without my dog I might as well be dead. I was screaming and my dad hit me, so I ran away. I didn't know where I was going, and I didn't care, I just wanted to get as far away as possible. Then this boy stopped me and made me smoke weed, and then it...happened."

A girl called Stella speaks out. "I got raped after someone gave me weed. I couldn't stop him, and I couldn't get away...I couldn't think straight."

Miss Tina nods. "That's one of the dangers of drinking alcohol and smoking weed; both make you less able to take care of yourself and keep yourself safe."

"I didn't care, though," I say. "I felt so bad that nothing seemed to matter. My dog was dead."

"How did you feel about your mother leaving?" Miss Tina asks me.

I can feel my jaw tense up in anger. "She hadn't left, they'd just had a fight, that's all. He killed my dog after just a stupid fight. They were always fighting." I feel so angry, that I'm glad he's not here because I'd want to kill him. "When I got back home, Mom was there at the house and I went crazy."

"I'm not surprised," Miss Tina says. "What did she say?"

"She said she'd buy me another one, like he didn't matter at all, like he was just a *thing*. I didn't want another one; I just wanted *him*. But that didn't happen as she left the next day for good with another man."

Freddie coughs, and says, "Sounds like she thinks she can throw things away and just buy a new one and it'll be all right. Is that what she does with people?"

"That's what it feels like," I say. "That's exactly what it feels like," and I feel admiration for my new friend who is only two years older than me yet seems so smart.

Miss Tina starts to speak. "It seems to me that there were other things going on between your mom and dad that had nothing to do with you or your dog. It's something we'll look at a little more deeply another day. You've all worked hard today. How did it feel, Melody, to share your thoughts and feelings with all of us? Did you feel safe and respected?"

I nod and say "Yes," because I do. I've never spoken so much in all my life, particularly to strangers. I don't have anyone to talk to, yet today I talked about things that are buried deep inside my heart and it feels fine.

"Well, I'm glad that you feel safe and respected because that's what we want for all of you at Beach Haven." She looks around the room. "Thanks for making Melody feel welcome and safe enough to talk about her problems."

I smile and my tears have gone. I look shyly around the group and something is happening to me that's never happened before—I feel a connection to other people. It feels scary, but exciting as well.

The next morning I'm in my shower. When I come out of my room Miss Tina says, "Melody, you have the most beautiful voice I've ever heard." My face is red.

"You have," Freddie says.

"Was I singing?" I ask.

"Girl, were you singing?"

I didn't realize. I've always had a song in my head but I didn't realize that I was singing out loud. No one's ever told me that I've got a nice voice before, and I feel shy but warm inside.

We all go into the Group Room and sit in a circle again.

Miss Tina starts to talk.

"Today we're going to look at being alone. What does being alone mean to you?"

She glances around the room.

"It depends," Paul says, frowning at her.

"On what?"

"On lots of things. If I want to be quiet, then I like being alone but if I feel *lonely*, then it feels horrible."

"Yeah," smiles Tammy, "I have to share a bedroom with my sisters and I long to be alone."

"Doesn't it depend on how you're feeling inside?" Rick asks.

"What do you mean?" Miss Tina asks.

"Well, I like my own company so I like being alone, but when I think of Jenny I feel so alone that it's unbearable."

I assume that Jenny must be his girlfriend and they've split up.

"So the way you react to being alone depends on how you're feeling at the time and also how you feel about yourself, is that right?" Miss Tina asks.

Rick looks at her and nods. "I guess so."

"Melody, what are your thoughts about being alone?"

I feel my face flush. I don't want to say, but everyone looks at me and so I feel as if I have to.

"I've always felt alone, apart from when I was with Buster, that's my dog. Even when Mom and Dad were home, and Danny too, my twin brother, I felt alone. We didn't talk to each other."

"What about at school?" Miss Tina presses me.

"That was ten times worse," I say, feeling a sudden urge to cry, and not being able to stop the tears from seeping out of my eyes. "No one bothered with me at home but at least they didn't bully me. At school I'm bullied every minute of every day."

I tell them about being a nerd in the front row and about the girls who gang together and make my life miserable.

"Do you want to hang out with them?" Miss Tina asks as I blow my nose noisily.

"Not really," I falter, "they're not very nice, in fact, they're mean, but it seems that if you're not in with them, they'll make your life a living hell."

A girl looks at me and nods. "That's how it is for me, too."

I can't help it but the first thing I think of is whether she's pretty or not...she's pretty, and then I don't get it. If she were at my school she'd be in the back row with the in-crowd. Why is she saying that she knows what it's like to be bullied at school?

"The girls at school wanted me in their gang and I felt..." she looks down at the floor, "...I felt flattered and a bit relieved. I didn't want to be left out, or suffer what the kids in the front row suffered, so I did everything I could to fit in with them. It kind of felt like I'd be protected if I were one of them. In a strange sort of way I felt *forced* to follow them, although no one made me...I just felt safer being in with them rather than...well, you know...on the outside."

I know what's she's trying to say; she's trying to say that it was better to be in with the girls in the back row, even though they were mean, than to be a nerd in the front row. I look at her and my feelings are mixed. I want to hate her for being the type of girl who makes my life miserable, yet I can hear pain in her voice, like she knows what it's like to suffer at the hands of those girls, too. I feel confused.

"So are you saying that you were afraid to be alone?" Miss Tina asks her.

She sits in silence for a moment and then looks at Miss Tina, and says, "I don't think I was afraid to be alone but I think I was afraid of what those girls could do to me if I wasn't in with them. Does that make sense?"

"What d'you think, Melody, does it make sense to you?"

My head's spinning and I don't know what to say.

Rick jumps in and as he talks I look at him with admiration.

"I think that school is like being in a jungle where the fittest survive and the rest suffer. Kids band together through fear of being the one in the front row that gets bullied...no one wants to go through that and so they stick together. I think it's sick, because if you were to ask each kid, most would say that they didn't want to be with kids that're mean, but they're just too scared to stand up for themselves and stand alone...they're scared that they'll get bullied, too."

He shakes his head and looks at Miss Tina.

"Honestly, it really is like a jungle at school. You have to fit in, be the same as everyone else, or you'll get picked on. I think it's crap, oops, sorry, but that's how it is. Everyone's so fake, so busy fitting in, so busy trying not to get bullied by the in-crowd. I don't give a..." He shakes his head. "I don't care. They can't hurt me..."

He seems so strong; he knows how it is but he doesn't care. I wish I felt that way.

Freddie speaks out, "Yeah, but that's you, Rick, maybe you're stronger than the rest of us. What if it really matters to you to fit in...being alone would feel awful."

Rick shrugs like he doesn't care.

I know what she means because I've longed to fit in, just like Danny does. He doesn't have any of the problems I have because he's in the in-crowd.

"Well, I guess so," Rick says, "I guess it's like Miss Tina says, it has to do with how you feel about yourself inside."

I listen and my stomach churns. I don't feel good about myself at all.

"What do kids do to cope with not being in the in-crowd, to protect themselves?" Miss Tina asks, looking at us.

"Band together?" Paul says.

I don't say anything because I'm ashamed. I don't think he's right, because most nerds don't want to be associated with other nerds. I remember the spotty guy who picked up my pencil in class...I thought he was a bigger nerd than me and so I'd be scared to be around anyone like him in case the bullies picked on me even more.

Freddie says, "Find just one person to hang around with."

Miss Tina nods.

"Some kids will try to buy their way into the in-crowd," Tammy says. "They do what they have to, to be accepted."

"Like what?" Miss Tina presses.

"Please them...do what they want."

"Like what?" she asks again.

"Well, it's virtually impossible to be accepted by the girls if they don't like you, but if you want to be accepted by the boys you have to give them what they want, and that's sex. It's sick but that's how it is."

"You give sex to be accepted by the boys in the back row?" Miss Tina asks, raising an eyebrow.

Several kids murmur "Yes," and I glance around, feeling safer than I've ever felt before, because these kids know what I've been through.

Tammy looks Miss Tina in the eye and says, "You've got no idea how bad it is at school if you don't belong, or if you're alone, or different."

"Yeah, but if you felt okay about yourself inside you wouldn't feel the need to do anything just to be accepted by the in-crowd...who cares about them?" Rick says. "What about your self-respect?"

"You're a guy; it's different for girls," Tammy says.

"Is it?" Miss Tina asks. "I think it's probably the same for girls and guys. I think Rick has the answer... how you feel about being excluded from the in-crowd depends upon how you feel about yourself inside. If you have self-respect, if you believe in yourself, then being separate from the in-crowd won't matter so much, and you won't feel you have to do things that will rob you of your self-respect in order to be accepted. Having low self-esteem leaves you feeling vulnerable and less able to cope with standing alone or being bullied."

I feel miserable. I don't feel good about myself; I have *no* self-esteem and I have no self-respect either. I had sex with those two guys in order to try to fit in, to be accepted, and to not feel alone. I feel so stupid. Why couldn't I have been my own person, to be comfortable being alone, to hold my head up high and walk away from the kids who bully me, to not care when they hurt my feelings? If I felt better about myself perhaps I could do those things, but I can't.

Miss Tina smiles at us. "Let's move on. I want to read you a story to help you understand loneliness and how you can be taken advantage of when you're feeling vulnerable. It's called 'The Golden Purse.' I hope you like it."

• • • •

Far, far away in the land that bobbed in and out of view depending upon the sea mist, there lived a young shepherd girl who tended her sheep on a hillside overlooking a town. She had no friends for she had to spend all her time taking care of her sheep, making sure that they didn't wander along high ledges or fall into deep ravines. Her sheep were her friends and she knew each one by name, for they were very special, a rare breed, whose wool was the color of golden corn. Every evening as the sun slid down over the hill, each sheep cast a soft golden shadow over the grass.

Although she loved them, every one, she longed to hear the sound of laughter and to know the joy of friendship with another human being.

"I love you, my friends," she said, stroking their wool, "but I need someone to talk to."

They licked her face and she laughed, but sadness rested in her heart.

High up on the hillside that evening in her little hut she spun the sheep's golden wool into thread by candlelight, and after eating her supper of goat cheese and bread, she began knitting golden sweaters to sell at the town's market place. She had a pile of sweaters that she'd already made and every few weeks she would journey down the hillside into the town to buy the goods she needed with the money she made from her knitting.

As she walked through the town, people flocked

around her to see what she'd brought, for her sweaters were spoken of in every town for a hundred miles; everyone wanted one. They nagged at her to sell them cheaply on the street, but she pushed forward and walked into the market place where she sat at her little stall and laid out her wares.

"Me first," a woman shouted, nudging everyone out of the way.

"I was here first," another woman argued.

"She always lets me have the first one," someone else said. "I'm her friend."

The young shepherd girl looked perplexed for she didn't have any friends; who was this person saying she was her friend? She didn't even know who had said it, for there were so many people scrambling to get to the front of the line to buy her sweaters.

They were gone within minutes and suddenly her stall was empty. She was alone and no one had said anything to her other than, "How much?"

With a heavy heart she bought her goods and trudged back up the hillside to her beloved sheep, who welcomed her without words.

That night she didn't knit another sweater. Instead she knitted a fine golden purse in which to put all the money she'd made from selling her sweaters, and stayed up long into the night until it was finished.

"Beautiful," she said to herself. "Just beautiful," and she put all the coins into it for safekeeping.

Weeks went past and she talked to her sheep to stave off the loneliness she felt, and through their wordless bleating she imagined what it would be like to have a friend, one that would share jokes and funny stories, and talk to her.

Her sadness at being alone filled her heart so much that she made a special trip down the hillside into the town and sold yet more of her sweaters to those who pushed and shoved to get to the front of the line.

Not one person had bothered to ask her how she was or how her sheep were doing, not one, and as her loneliness threatened to overwhelm her, she decided not to go straight back up the hillside, for she was desperate to talk to another human being. Looking around her, everyone was too busy and didn't seem to notice her, so she walked over to the local tavern and pushed the heavy oak door open.

It was dark and everyone turned around to see who was coming through the door. She felt her face flush with anxiety, but she forced herself on and walked up to the bartender.

"Please, may I have a glass of lemonade," she said, and as she opened her golden purse, suddenly she was surrounded by people all wanting to talk to her. Her face was flushed with pleasure; someone wanted to be her friend at last, and one by one she bought each of them a glass of lemonade until all her money was gone.

She stood alone with her empty golden purse. Everyone had gone back to their seats, drinking the lemonade she'd bought them, but not one wanted to stand and talk to her once they'd gotten what they wanted from her. She had given everything and yet she was still alone with no one to talk to.

Tears sprung into her eyes and she ran out of the tavern, down the main street, past the deserted market place, and began to climb the steep hillside. She was sobbing with pain and loneliness by the time she had reached a ledge that ran around the hill, and there she stumbled into a traveler wending his way from town to town.

"Why are you crying?" he asked her.

She sobbed as she told him of her loneliness and how she'd hoped that if she'd had a golden purse full of money, she could find friends who would talk to her.

"The world is full of greed and trickery," he said, "but do not let that blind you to what goodness there is in people. You just have to be selective, for if you open your golden purse you will attract all those who are filled with greed, and whose hearts are shallow."

"Are you saying that I shouldn't give to people then?" she asked him.

"Oh, no, not at all. Sharing is the most wonderful thing in the world, for no one can truly grow without sharing and learning from one another, but

you must be selective. Do not stand with your golden purse open for all those to see what's inside, and to rob you of everything you have and hold dear. Stand among them with your golden purse closed. Then when someone stands beside you who truly wants to talk to you and know the truths in your heart, open your golden purse and share what you have."

She dried her eyes and carried on up the hill towards the only friends she knew and rested from the experience.

She spun the golden wool into thread and knitted sweater after sweater and soon she had another pile to take to the market place in the town.

Stroking each of her golden sheep as she left, she made her way back down to the town, with her head held high. She ignored the crowd that tried to get her to sell her sweaters before she got to the market place, to buy them cheaply and cheat her of her worth, and she remained firm and resolute.

The sweaters were sold in a few moments and her golden purse was full of money, so she walked to the tavern and opened the door.

The bartender said, "The usual, Ma'am?"

"Yes, please," she said, "one of your fine lemonades, if you please," and suddenly the room was full of the sound of chairs scraping against the stone floor, as virtually everyone rushed towards her and her golden purse.

She stood with her head held high, her chin jutting

out in determination, remembering the stranger's words. Her purse was closed and she stared ahead at the bartender, as he passed comment on the weather and asked her how her sheep were doing. As she kept her golden purse closed, little by little the crowd around her whittled away, leaving her alone.

She felt confused, for she'd done what the stranger had said, yet she was still alone with no one to talk to; the bartender was busy and had gone on to someone else to pass comment on the weather as he poured their lemonade. She felt uncomfortable, and loneliness crept upon her like a chilling morning mist, making her long to race back up the hillside to the comfort of her silent sheep, but something made her stand still. It was the stranger who had said, "If you stand there with your golden purse closed and protected, those who long to talk to you, to know your stories and your truth, will come forward and then, only then, can you open your purse and share as much as you want to."

She ignored the discomfort, although it felt more terrible than she had ever imagined, for she felt that those she'd rebuffed were back in their seats talking about her and laughing at her loneliness.

She sipped her lemonade until there was just a shimmer at the bottom of her glass, and just as her resolve was about to take flight and she was about to run out of the tavern, someone tapped her on the shoulder.

"You're the shepherd girl that makes those wonderful sweaters, aren't you? I bought one to give to my mother and she loves it. Can I buy you a lemonade, please?"

The young shepherd girl flushed with pleasure, and didn't need to open her golden purse since the man opened his own purse. And as they sat there talking through the night, sharing each other's stories and truths, she opened her golden purse only when she wanted to, and no more or less than he did.

Chapter Four

I sigh, I know I do. That story is about me, I know it is. I want to cry but I manage not to. I know what it feels like to have no friends and people who only want me for sex, not for me, for who I really am.

Miss Tina smiles at all of us. "Cute, isn't it. Did you like it? Do you understand it? It'll probably mean different things to each of you. What are your thoughts about it? What do you think the purse represents?"

Freddie says, "I think that the purse could be several things: Her self-respect, her friendship, affections, or sex."

"I think so, too," Miss Tina said. "Well done. What do you think the sweaters represented?"

"The same?"

"Say more."

"Well, things that people wanted from her. I suppose it could mean her talents; after all she made them, so she had talents."

"It could have represented something that she had to give that keeps you warm, because sweaters keep you warm."

"There are no right or wrong answers," Miss Tina says. "The point of the story is to make you think and to help you apply it to your own situation."

Julie says, "It showed me that when the girl was lonely she let people take advantage of her, like my boyfriend did when I was feeling vulnerable."

Miss Tina nodded. "Can you see how easily it can happen? The young shepherd girl was lonely and wanted friends; she didn't really do anything to deserve the way those people in the tavern treated her. Her loneliness, and perhaps her inexperience, blinded her to the fact that some human beings can be greedy and self-centered."

Rick sounds angry. "You make it sound like all boys are just after one thing—sex—but not all of us are like that, you know."

"That's right," Miss Tina says. "They're not, but some are. Are you saying that you are the sort of guy who came up to the shepherd girl at the end of the story?"

He goes a bit red. "I've got lots of friends that are girls and I haven't tried to have sex with any of them, nor would I."

He sounds angry.

I can feel my face getting redder and redder. I blurt out, "I know how the shepherd girl felt, especially when she gave them everything and they all sat and laughed at her. That's what happened to me. Those boys tricked me into giving them sex, then laughed at me afterwards."

Rick glares at me. "We're not all like that, Melody."

"I think that people are shallow and greedy," a girl says, who is usually quiet, "and I think it's better to be alone and lonely than to have people taking advantage of you, so that you lose your self-respect."

Miss Tina says, "The story shows how bad the shepherd girl felt when she'd been taken advantage of. It also shows how uncomfortable she felt when she was determined that she wouldn't be taken advantage of again. Do you think that she was brave to hold her head up high, keeping her self-respect, even though when she returned to the tavern to face the people who had used her, she was hurting and felt very lonely?"

"Yes," I murmur. "If it were me I'd have run out of there; I don't think I could have stood it to hear those men jeering at me...I'm scared to go back to school," I say, as an afterthought.

Freddie says, "But the story shows us that even though the girl was hurt once she didn't give up. She wanted to make friends and tried again, but the second time she believed in herself and was more choosy. You can go back to school, Melody. Be the shepherd girl. Stand tall, they'll soon get fed up with picking on you if you show them that it doesn't bother you."

"I can't," I say, feeling stricken at the thought.

Miss Tina smiles at me gently. "Do you feel like you lost *your* self-respect, Melody, like the shepherd girl?"

I nod miserably.

"Y'know, wanting to be liked costs too much if you lose everything you're worth, your self-respect, but if that's happened to you then you can always get it back by changing your behavior and the way you think. The shepherd girl was humiliated when she thought all those people liked her but all they wanted her for was to buy them a lemonade; she had opened her purse to everyone, but she changed her behavior and the way she thought, and then got her self-respect back again. You can do that too, Melody."

Freddie's nodding at me, and so are the others. I give them a weak smile.

Freddie says, "My mom and dad say that it's not a good idea to have sex before you're married, and I've just thought of something else that's in the story. The shepherd girl was trying to get to the market place with her valuable sweaters, but people kept trying to make her sell them cheaply. They were trying to cheat her—they didn't want to pay the full price for the sweaters. And that could be the same as men trying to get you to have casual sex with them without the commitment of a real relationship or marriage."

"Well done, Freddie," Miss Tina says. "I hadn't noticed that, but you're quite right."

My head is full of thoughts. Can I get my self-respect back? Can I find friends? I hope so, but right now I'd rather be the young shepherd girl up on the hill with sheep for friends than go back to school where everyone is laughing at me.

"You've all done really well today. Let's stop. It's Friday, and you all know what that means, don't you?"

I don't.

"It's Show Night, so I know you'll all be wanting to go and work on what you're going to do this evening. I can't wait. Off you go. See you all later."

"What's Show Night?" I ask Freddie.

"Every Friday we put on a show where everyone does something."

I feel a sudden wave of panic.

"But I can't do anything."

"Are you kidding? You can sing."

"I can't sing in front of anyone," I say, feeling panic rising in my throat.

"Of course you can, just pretend you're in the shower," she grins at me.

"I can't."

"You have to, it's part of the program here. It's

a safe place, remember, a place where you can do something, anything, no matter how small, and it'll be okay."

"What did you do last Friday?"

She laughs, "Oh, it was fun. One of the girls—she's gone now—and I did a mime. I was pretending to be her reflection in the mirror. It was so funny. I had a hard time stopping myself from laughing, especially when she started popping spots on her chin and I had to do the same, and try to pull the same face. Really, Melody, it's fun."

"What're you going to do tonight then?"

"I think I might do a jive with Tammy. You don't have to do it on your own, you can work with someone."

Instantly I feel left out and worthless; I know no one'll want to work with me.

"Rick plays guitar. Why don't you ask him if he'll play while you sing?"

"I couldn't."

"Oh, don't be silly. Hey Rick..." she calls, as he passes us down the hall. "You can play for Melody tonight, can't you?"

"What d'you want to sing?" he asks me.

I can't believe that he'll actually consider it.

"Um, I don't know, what can you play?"

"I'll leave you two to it," Freddie says, and she walks away, leaving me blushing and tongue-tied.

We're allowed the whole afternoon off so Rick says

that we can practice together. He gets his guitar from his room and I follow him outside; we sit on a bench in the playground while he strums. I recognize some of the things he's playing but not all, and as he says, "Do you know this?" I shake my head. I start to feel really useless and scared that he'll walk off, thinking I'm rubbish. I don't know what to suggest. I don't know what I know or don't know. My head's in a spin. I've never been with a boy that wanted to be with me, even if it's only to put on a show. I don't know what to do.

There are kids near us and I can hear them whispering, trying to keep their ideas secret from us, yet they're close enough to hear what we're saying.

"C'mon," Rick says, "Let's move away."

I follow him down to the beach and when he sits down I sit next to him. The sun is shining and my face feels warm. Sitting here feels so different from anything I've ever felt in my life; it feels peaceful and calm as the waves roll gently up the sand and stop a few feet away from us. I know that he doesn't *like* me, like *that*, but this feels like heaven to me, sitting next to someone who wants to be with me.

"D'you know any Elvis songs?"

I know my face lights up; my mom and dad love Elvis and I've grown up listening to him blaring throughout our house. Rick starts singing, "You ain't nothin' but a hound dog" and strumming his guitar fast. I grin at him but am too shy to sing along even though I know the words.

"C'mon, sing with me," he says breathlessly as he's strumming.

So I try, awkwardly at first, and as he doesn't laugh at me I do what Freddie told me to do...pretend that I'm in the shower and I sing along with him.

"Cool," he says, as we finish. "You really do have a great voice, Melody. What else do you know?"

I shrug. "Most of his stuff, I guess. My mom and dad loved him."

He strums and my heart leaps. I know what it is.

"Love me tender, love me true, never let me go," he sings, and I join in, although I don't know how I hold myself together because I think my heart is about to burst with happiness. I know he's not singing it to me but it's still the best moment of my life.

He looks at me when we finish, he's strangely quiet, but I don't know what his eyes are saying. I suddenly feel sick and I don't know what to say, nor does he for a moment, then he looks away towards the waves that are getting closer and closer to us.

"Tide's coming in, we'd better move back a bit."

We shift back a few feet.

"How old are you?" he asks me.

"Fourteen. How old are you?" I ask bravely.

"Seventeen."

He seems so grown up to me and I feel shy and silly.

"D'you know what I think we should do, seeing as this is a place that helps us with the pain in our lives? I think we should sing about pain." He suddenly seems excited.

I feel totally stupid because I don't know what he's getting at.

He looks at me and suddenly seems serious.

"I was really listening to what you said about those two guys who used you, and I know you were hurt. I meant what I said about not all guys being like that. How about we do two songs, one about how angry you feel—we can change some of the words to 'You ain't nothin' but a hound dog' so that it fits—and the second one about what you really want, well, what everyone wants...to be loved...'Love me tender.' What d'you think? Then it wouldn't be just us singing and playing; it would mean something."

I can't believe that he's saying all this. I can't believe that he's this smart; I'd never have thought of it. I nod, too full to speak.

"Right, that's what we'll do. I'll introduce it and play, but you do the singing, okay?"

My head's spinning. Never, ever, in my life has anyone wanted me to do anything with them, or thought that what I can do is worth anything. I've never known that I *could* do anything. It feels really weird to have people say something nice about me.

Can I sing? So I sing in the shower, so what, that's just noise. I know I've always got a tune in my head, always, it stops me sleeping sometimes.

He's seventeen and seems so confident. He tells me what to do and when I get it wrong he barks at me, telling me to pay attention and get it right. I do, and as he pushes me all afternoon my nose gets sunburned.

We meet the others for dinner and everyone's excited. No one's saying what they're going to do tonight and it feels like Christmas Eve; the air of expectancy is suffocating.

I can't eat a thing but I watch in admiration as Freddie plows her way through everything on her plate, obviously not at all nervous about the show. I leave the dining room hungry but I'm not empty, be-cause I'm full to the brim with excitement, nerves, and infatuation.

We file into the living room, and Miss Tina and several other staff are there, all waiting with expec-tancy on their faces. I have a flash of nerves again and take a seat near the back of the room. Ricky winks at me, which doesn't help at all, in fact it makes me feel worse.

Stella does a magic card trick and leaves us all wondering. I clap loudly, praying that when it's my turn they'll clap really hard for me.

Paul stands out in front of us all and says, "I wrote this myself when I was thinking about everyone here and everyone in my life, people who have hurt me and people who have made me happy. He stands still for a moment and when everyone is silent he says, emphatically, "Friendship is as friendship does."

He bows almost immediately and we all clap, but I'm caught between a place that thinks, "Is that all, when I've put so much effort into this?" to a place that giggles along with the others when Miss Tina shouts out, "Well, that was short but sweet."

He bows again and laughs, saying, "Less is more," as he goes back to his seat.

Freddie and Tammy get up next and put on a CD, then they dance the way my mom and dad used to years ago. It looks great and I wish I knew how to do it. Freddie's twirling her around really fast and tries to swing her over her back but misses and they land in a heap on the floor. They make me laugh so much that I nearly wet myself.

Julie stands up and starts to read from a piece of paper.

"I wrote this the day after I got here...I hope you like it."

It's hard to be a kid sometimes
When life is falling apart
When Mom and Dad are fighting hard
And ignore my broken heart.

The house seems empty without Dad
It no longer seems as warm
Although my mom's still with us
I'm lost amidst this storm.

Her face is clouded with sorrow
She no longer looks at me
They're fighting over who gets me
I wish they'd just let it be.

There's no comfort in my family
So I'll have to look elsewhere
She doesn't even notice me
But my boyfriend, he is there.

I've given him something precious
Something he threw away
I learned that love cannot be bought
A truth that's with me today.

My mom and dad're still fighting
And I don't know how it'll end
But Beach Haven and its workers
Will always be my friend.

We all cheer really loudly and she smiles as she sits back down. Now it's our turn. My stomach's turned to jelly and I feel so sick that I can't breathe. I'll never be able to do it, but as Rick gets up I know I have to follow, for to chicken out would be more humiliating than singing poorly in front of people.

"This is a safe place, this is a safe place, this is a safe place," I tell myself over and over as I walk to the front of the room to stand next to Rick. I'm so grateful that he agreed to do this with me, because I couldn't have done it on my own.

I can't believe how confident he is; I feel like a wet lettuce leaf and I'm trembling.

He strums his guitar to make everyone quiet down, and I stand there wringing my hands.

"Well, we've got much the same message as Julie's poem. We didn't want to just sing, we wanted it to mean something, something that's about our therapy here. We've been working hard lately on buying friends, giving sex to try and buy a boyfriend or to be accepted by the in-crowd, so we thought that we'd sing one song that describes the kind of guys you girls don't want to get mixed up with. Then we're going to do a song about something that's on everyone's wish-list. And we only had today to practice, so please be nice, okay?"

He looks at me and smiles, nodding, with something on his face that says, "Don't mess up on me, now." My heart's racing; I can barely breathe. I'm scared to death and I smell bad, I know I do, my deodorant has just failed me. He looks at me and I feel sick but it's not just because I'm scared, it's because of the way he smiles at me. I feel paralyzed.

He leans forward and whispers in my ear, "Just pretend you're in the shower; let 'em have it, you'll be great."

He starts to play and there's a sea of faces in front of me, which I can't handle, so I turn to face him and force myself to be in my shower. I block everyone out except him and the music he's making; then he nods at me and I start to sing.

My voice is croaky at first because my throat is so choked with fear, but he's as loud as me so I don't feel alone and start to relax. He's smiling at me and I watch his fingers running over his guitar so that I'm in perfect time with him.

You ain't nothin' but a hound dog
Lying all the time
You ain't nothin' but a hound dog
Trying all the time,
To make me lose my honor
So you ain't no friend of mine.

You said that you loved me
But that was just a lie
You said that you wanted me
But that was just a lie
You took something precious
And made me wanna die...

I sing on and on, reading the new words from a paper in front of me, and as I watch his fingers on the guitar we end the song exactly together.

The kids are hooting and hollering, and my face is flushing. I did it; I did it!

He holds his hand up and they quiet down again.

"And now we'll do a song that's on everyone's wish-list."

He gives one strum, that's all, and I start. "Love me tender, love me true, never let me go..."

I'm in my shower, there's no one with me, just my longing to be loved, and I sing as if I'm alone. As my voice rings out I vaguely become aware that although Rick's standing next to me, he's stopped playing and I'm singing on my own.

I sing and I sing, and as I long to be loved for the person I am, with my hooked nose, sunken piggy eyes and crooked teeth, so it all comes out through my voice and the words of Elvis's song.

When I finish tears are prickling my eyes, but I don't feel sick anymore, just stunned. I can't believe I did it.

Rick's staring at me and it's a moment or two before everyone starts clapping, but when they do they just don't stop, and suddenly I'm embarrassed, as if they've seen straight down into my heart.

Rick puts his arm around me and gives me a hug. "You were fantastic," he says in my ear as the room is filled with noise, people cheering, all for me. I can't believe it.

Miss Tina comes forward and hugs me.

"You are beautiful, just beautiful," and I start to cry. No, not me. I'm not beautiful, I'm ugly. "I've never heard anything so beautiful," and she hugs me again.

Freddie and Tammy jump up and are hugging me, and my tears stop as excitement races through me. I did it; I can't believe I did it. I look at Rick and he's grinning at me, and in that moment I know I'm in love.

It's hard to calm down and I don't want to; today has been the best day of my whole life.

I can't eat my snack before bedtime and when Miss Tina sends us to bed, saying that it was the best Show Night ever, I can't get to sleep. I feel excited, really excited. What kind of place is this? I feel more alive than I've ever felt. I don't know where to go with the feeling. Suddenly my mom and dad seem very far away and, I hate to even think it, but they are completely insignificant to me. I want to stay here forever and never go home.

I toss and turn all night, and when the morning staff come and wake us up I'm just beginning to fall asleep. But even though I'm tired there's a thrill of energy rushing through me. I want to see Rick. I shower and try to ignore my hooked nose in the mirror and a voice in my head that threatens to bring me down.

I don't have any makeup, so as soon as I'm dressed I run down the hall and beg Freddie to do my makeup, to make my eyes stand out again.

"What's up?" she says. "Slow down, I'm tired; I'm not awake yet."

I feel like I'm my three-year-old cousin begging

for candy as I beg her to do my eyes, when I can tell that she doesn't really want to. I can't help it though; I'm on a mission, one that's as important as my little cousin's pursuit of candy.

She makes me look like someone else and I don't know how to thank her enough.

"Go away girl, and let me get ready myself," she says, laughing at me. She seems so grown up even though she's only two years older than me, and as I think about all she says and everything she knows, I want to be just like her. I want to be wise and confident. I want to know how to make the best of what I've been given. I still hate my mom for giving me this face, but my hatred doesn't feel so raw now that Freddie has shown me how to soften the sharp edges of my face. At this moment I can't decide whether I'm going to be a chef or a beautician when I grow up, or maybe I'll be a therapist like Miss Tina. I don't know what to think anymore. My thoughts are whizzing around my head with nowhere to land except on the presence of Rick. He's in my head the whole time, every minute of the day, and I can't think of anything other than him. I get into trouble at breakfast and in group for not paying attention, but I don't care, all I want is to feel everything I felt last night all over again, over and over again. I never want it to go away, ever.

He comes up to me in the dining room.

"You were amazing last night," he says, and I hear

in his voice that he likes me. Can it be true that he really likes me?

I don't know what to say and I fear that I'll make a fool of myself if I speak, yet if I don't he might walk off and I'll feel wretched all day.

"It's thanks to you," I gush.

He grabs my arm and suddenly looks serious.

"Listen to me. It was down to you. You sang that song without me. I didn't play anything other than the first few notes. You did it, you, not me. You have talent, girl, use it, sing. One of my cousins plays keyboard and the other plays lead guitar. When we get out of here, we should get together and form a band. You have a gift and if you don't use it, it'll be tragic, as tragic as the crap we've all been through in our lives so far."

He walks off and I'm stunned; stunned by what he's just said to me, ugly me. What's he talking about...a band? Don't be silly; no one would want me in their band. My feelings are in tatters.

He seems different from last night. He didn't notice my makeup, my eyes that Freddie has sculpted to reduce the shape of my nose. I feel deflated, and I want to run after him and tug on his jacket like my three-year-old cousin with a scraped knee, but I can't.

I follow the kids outside. I don't want to sit on the swings, I just want to go back twenty-four hours to being on the beach with Rick, practicing the music between us, but he's standing there talking to Paul and I'm amongst the girls. I feel alone and I don't want to listen to what they're talking about. I feel as if I'm a little boat set adrift, bobbing about in the sea of my emotions, and Rick is my wind, my tide, and my storm.

Chapter Five

It's the weekend and my mom comes to visit me.

"How are you?" she says, not looking me in the eye.

I want to shout at her and say just what I think of her, leaving us like that, but we're in the dining room and other parents are visiting their kids too, so I hold it in and say nothing.

Rick's at the other end of the room and lots of people are around his table.

"Are they treating you okay?" Mom asks.

I still say nothing.

"How could you, Melody, how could you try to kill yourself?" She has tears in her eyes and sniffs into a tissue.

I feel so angry with her. How can she ask me that and make me feel bad when it was because of her that I did it? If she hadn't left the first time, my dog would still be alive and I wouldn't have done what I did with those boys and suffered the humiliation at school. And she left anyway, leaving me with no one who cares. How dare she say, "How could you?"

Rick looks over at me just as I'm about to explode, room full of parents or not, and he smiles at me. My anger just melts away and, as he looks away, I look back at Mom and say, "Why'd you leave, Mom?"

She looks down at the table for a moment before digging in her bag for her cigarettes. Her hands are shaking.

"I had to," she says, "I couldn't take anymore."

"You can't smoke in here," I tell her, feeling as if I'm the parent and she's the child. "Didn't you think about me and Danny?"

"I did, I did, that's why I left, so that you wouldn't have to suffer all the arguments anymore."

Now I feel like she's trying to make me feel as if she's done me a favor...this feels like a game of Ping-Pong, with my emotions being the ball.

"Dad killed my dog because you left," I state, just short of shouting.

She looks at me and there's something in her face that looks like...I don't know...is it pain? I think it might be. She reaches out to take my hand and although I'd rather push her away to make her pay for what's she's done, I don't.

"Baby, I don't know how to make it better. I don't know what to do. If I say what's on my mind, you'll think I'm being hateful about your dad, and I don't want to get into all of that mess, but if I stay quiet then you'll blame me unjustly."

I don't know what she's talking about; she's talking in riddles.

"Try me," I say, with my face set.

She coughs and takes a gulp of coffee.

"It's been a mess for ages. I've tried to keep it from you both but I guess you both knew."

Well, actually we didn't, or I didn't, I don't know about Danny. You see, no one in our family talks to each other so I have no idea what Danny knew, or what Dad was feeling, nor Mom...we were like little islands, totally disconnected.

I shake my head. "We don't talk in our family," I say, not meaning to be sarcastic but realizing that I sound spiteful.

"I'm sorry," she says.

I shrug. "Go on."

"I'm sorry to tell you this but your dad has been playing around for years, and I've always put up with it because I didn't want to end up divorcing like my parents did. But one day it all came to a head after I walked in on him in our bed with another woman. Something just snapped inside me."

I'm listening intently and I can't ignore what she's saying because part of me knows she's telling the truth, because he brought that woman home the day Mom left and didn't care at all that I saw her in their bed. I look at her and she's got tears in her eyes, so I take her hand.

"This has been going on for years; I should have taken both of you and left him years ago but I didn't know what to do for the best, so I stayed. I wanted to do things differently from my parents and look what I've done...just the same—hurt my kids like my parents hurt me."

She blows her nose and I say nothing; I don't know what to say.

"Donnie at work has been after me for years but I've always stayed faithful, always; you have to believe me, Melody. But something died in me the day I walked in on him in our bed with someone else. I gave up. I told Donnie what had happened and that's when our relationship started. I shouldn't have, because two wrongs don't make a right, but everything I'd tried to do to keep our family together just fell apart that day."

I feel confused. So why'd he kill my dog? It doesn't fit and I say so. I can feel my face twisted with pain.

"To hurt you," she says, with as much pain on her face as there is on mine. "To turn you away from me. If he killed the dog and blamed it on my leaving, it would be my fault and you'd hate me. I'm so sorry, Melly, I hate to have to tell you what your father's really like."

She hasn't called me by my baby name for years

and it reaches deep inside me to a place where there was only her and me together. I should stand up and stop her from speaking about my dad like that, only I can't, for I know she's telling the truth. I've been on the end of his spite countless times but I just thought it was me being difficult or stupid, and that I deserved to be treated that way. I've always known that I'm no good; his face has told me so.

"There was no reason to kill my dog," I sniff, and I hate it but tears roll down my face, and I try to hide them in case Rick should look over at me. "*I* took care of my dog. He said that because you'd left us, he wouldn't be able to manage with two kids and a dog, so he had no choice but to kill my dog. *I* took care of my dog, not him, not you, not Danny. *Me!*"

She squeezes my hand so tightly that I can feel her trembling through my fingers.

"I know, I know. Don't you see, it was his way of getting back at me?"

"Why you? You didn't care about my dog; how could that get back at you?"

"Melly, I love you so much; to lose you would be the worst thing that could ever happen to me, and if you thought it was through me that you lost your dog, I'd lose you. Can you see the way his mind works?"

I pull my hand away from hers and bury my face in my hands to hide the tears that are running down my face. It's sick, really sick, and if she's right, and deep down I know she is, I hate the fact that half of me comes from somebody as cruel as that. I start to sob as a realization dawns on me...I've always hated my mother's genes, for her sunken piggy eyes, hooked nose and crooked teeth, when really the genes I should have hated were the spiteful, nasty genes of a person who could kill an animal just to get back at another human being. Suddenly I hate it that I have his "pretty," full lips.

Rick is by my side looking concerned.

"Mel, are you okay?"

He takes my hand and leads me out to the playground. I can see my mom sitting at the table through the window as we sit on the swings and I tell him what she's just said.

"That's hateful, if it's true. Do you believe her? I mean when parents get divorced they can say some nasty stuff about each other in order to score points, if you know what I mean."

I nod. "It's all true, I know it is. I just haven't wanted to face it before. He's mean, really mean." I tell him about waking up and finding a woman in their bed the night Mom had left. "He didn't care about me or what I might be feeling. I know she's telling me the truth."

We sway on the swings, talking and working stuff out.

My mom walks towards us and I can see that she's been crying really hard. Rick stands up and holds out his hand.

"I'm Rick, Ma'am. Your daughter has the most beautiful voice I've ever heard."

She smiles at him and looks at me with a plea on her face.

"Melly?"

I stand up and push the swing away and go into her arms.

"I believe you, Mom, I do. I don't blame you about my dog, but it just hurts so bad," and then I'm crying again.

She holds me tight and croons in my ear, and I feel that I should be embarrassed behaving this way in front of Rick, but as my chin rests on my mom's shoulder I can see him smiling sympathetically at me, like he really cares.

She leaves and I feel sad and confused.

On weekends there's not much to do so we chill out, watch movies, walk along the beach, play Ping-Pong, or bake cookies. Freddie, Rick and I walk along the beach and sit crossed-legged facing the ocean.

"I don't know what to think," I say. "I know my mom's telling me the truth but I don't know what to do with the anger I feel towards my dad for what he did. I also feel...um...I think I feel...dirty."

"Dirty?" Freddie asks, frowning.

"Yes, dirty. I don't want to accept that I'm half him. I don't want to think that someone who could do such a thing is part of who I am."

"Yeah, but, hang on a minute," Rick says, lying

back onto the sand and resting on his elbow. "You may have both their genes but you are you. You don't need to feel that, because your father is a piece of dirt, you are, or could ever be. You are your own person, never mind who made you. Would you think the same way if you'd been adopted? You wouldn't know who had made you; all you'd have is yourself and what you choose to be. So why would it be any different just because you *do* know who made you and one of those people was rotten? You are you, not them, and you can be who you want to be."

Freddie's smiling at me and nods. "He's right, girl. Come here, have a hug."

I start crying again; I've always longed for a big sister and wish it could be Freddie.

We walk back to Beach Haven for dinner and then sit through a movie that ends before I've got the plot, for my mind's elsewhere.

I toss and turn in my bed, longing to go to sleep because I feel exhausted, but my mom's words haunt me and I'm scared about what will happen to me. I can't go home. I can't be anywhere near that man. I want to be with my mom, but I realize that I don't even know where she's living. I don't know her phone number either.

Sleep keeps trying to evade me, and just as I float off something snaps me back to the reality of my bed and the waves crashing outside beyond the playground. A figure with no face floats by me while I'm in the dining room. Every time I drift off to sleep the figure's there. I get up and ask for a drink.

"What's the matter, Melody, can't you sleep?" the night staff ask me.

"No."

"You had a visit with your mom today, didn't you? How'd it go?"

"Okay, but she told me some stuff that hurt. She said that my dad killed my dog to spite her, to turn me away from her, and I know she's not lying. I don't know what to do. I can't go home. I never want to see my dad again, I hate him."

"Oh, sweetheart, try not to worry. It'll all work out; just wait and see."

I go back to bed not at all reassured; I don't know if it'll all work out. I'm not going home to live with my dad ever again, and if they make me then I'm going to run away. I want to live with Rick, and as I nestle into my bed and begin to dream of him, the figure slides into my mind again but just out of view. I shake my head and concentrate on Rick and his smile.

On Sundays they have a church service and we have to go. I sit there feeling abandoned, immersed in thoughts of how I can contact my mom while others pray out loud. I'm expected to say "Amen" and do so a fraction or so later than everyone else. Rick's hair is sticking up all over the place and it doesn't look as if he's combed it...I want to laugh. He catches my eye and grins. All my thoughts about my mom disappear in an instant and my mind and body are full of thoughts of Rick, and I only feel mildly ashamed that I should be thinking about Jesus. I wonder if Jesus ever fell in love; I hope so because then He'd know what's in my heart this very minute.

Dinner's good. Miss Tina's on duty and she insists that we set the table as if it were Christmas. She's hot on manners, too. I love her; she makes me laugh.

We shake out crisp white tablecloths over our normally bare tables and she shows us how to place the silverware, napkins and glasses. Each Sunday we take turns serving each other. Today it's the boys' turn to serve the girls...I like it. The food is just regular food but Miss Tina makes it special; it feels like Thanksgiving and to me it *is* Thanksgiving, for I am thankful to be here and get the help that all the staff have given me, and I'm thankful for Rick and Freddie. I don't know how to leave here. I never want to leave; the thought of leaving fills me with fear.

"Carrots, Madam?" Rick says, bowing low, and I giggle.

"Just a few."

"Oh, have some more—they help you see in the dark, and we all know what darkness feels like, don't we? So have some more carrots, lots of them."

Paul walks behind him, saying, "She's not a rabbit, y'know."

I'm scared for a minute thinking that he's making fun of my crooked teeth, but as he walks about serving peas, I can see that he's not being mean to me, and I'm just being too sensitive.

Finally the boys have served all of us girls so they serve themselves. Miss Tina makes us use the right knives and forks, even though we usually only have forks. She teaches us manners "so that we'll know what to do in the future if prospective employers take us out to dinner and decide to judge us by our table manners." Mine are pretty good because both Mom and Dad would get on us about eating with our mouths shut and not talking with our mouths full.

We have dessert, which the boys have to serve, and sip lemonade from our glasses, placed at strategic places on the tablecloth in front of each of us.

I'm stuffed, really stuffed. I don't usually eat this much but it seems rude to say "No" when the boys are making so much effort to be attentive and polite.

We all help clear the tables and leave them spotless; it's part of our "growing," Miss Tina says. I'm so stuffed that I need to do some "resting" now.

It's nearly time for visitation again and I prepare myself for a lonely afternoon; my mom came yesterday so I'm not expecting anyone. I'm surprised when Miss Tina calls me.

"Your dad's here with your brother, too."

I don't want to go to the dining room. I want to see Danny but not my dad, but I don't want to cause a scene and have Miss Tina think poorly of me. So I go to the dining room and there they are, sitting by the window that looks out over the beach. I know that Danny will be excited, not having been to the beach before.

I walk up to them and instantly I can feel the tension, like cobwebs brushing across the hairs on my arm on a hot summer night. Danny turns his attention away from the beach outside the window and looks at me, but doesn't know what to say...nor do I.

Dad looks at me. "Well, what have you got to say for yourself, eh?"

I look at him and instantly his attitude makes me sick. What have *I* got to say for myself? I've got plenty to say but because I know that Danny has to go home with him, I hold it all in. Why should Danny have to pay for my honesty? However, the sight of him and his defensiveness, even after what he's done to my precious dog, makes me more sick than I can say, so I stand up.

"C'mon," I say to Danny quietly, "let's go."

"Suit yourself. I didn't have to come here, you know; it cost me money to get here," Dad says and immediately turns around and starts flirting with Tammy's mom who's sitting at the next table.

I show Danny around and all he can say is "Cool" over and over.

I push the door open to the playground and some of the kids are out there hanging around. "C'mon," I say to Danny.

Freddie's already out there.

"My folks didn't show; no big deal," she says trying to hide her hurt. "Who's this?"

"This is my brother, my twin brother, Danny."

"Cool," she says. "You have a remarkable sister. Do you know that she can sing better than anyone I've ever heard before? She brought the house down on Show Night."

I wish she'd be quiet; I'm a nerd, that's how my brother thinks of me. I feel embarrassed; the nice things she's saying about me don't fit while my brother and father are present. I can't be that person Freddie and Rick see me as when I'm around my dad and brother, because they only know me as the ugly, nerdy, piggy eyed, hooked nose and crooked teeth, Melody. It makes me want to run far away from Danny, for he is part of my old life and I want to get rid of it; I want to be the person everybody sees in me here at Beach Haven. But as I look at Danny and realize he's part of the life I want to get rid of, I know that I don't want to get rid of *him*, for there's something in his face that reminds me of me and my pain. We're twins; can he know my pain, can he?

"I know, I've heard her in the shower," he says, and I'm stunned that he would've noticed me singing, but I'm more rocked that he would think something good about me and say it out loud.

We sit on a bench with Freddie.

"Mom came yesterday," I say.

"Did she?" his face lights up. "What did she say?"

"She told me things about her and Dad that we don't know. Did you know that he's been running around with other women for years?"

He's quiet, but nods.

"You knew? How?"

"I've seen him with other women in his car around town."

"Did you tell Mom?"

"No, of course not. I didn't want her to be hurt."

He sits quietly for a moment and then says, "I was scared, too, because although we've always been poor, if Dad left we would've been even poorer and I didn't want Mom to have to work even harder than she does now."

"Why didn't you tell me?"

He shrugs. "I don't mean anything by it, Mel, but you might have told Mom, then either he would leave or she would."

I sit there feeling a twinge of anger that he shut me out but as soon as it flashes through me it's gone, and it dawns on me just how isolated each of us was in our family, all for different reasons. He was trying to hold the family together so that Mom wouldn't suffer, Mom was trying to hide how she was feeling so that we wouldn't suffer, Dad didn't care about any of us, and I was locked in my own little world being an ugly nerd.

"Mom told me that she put up with him because she didn't want to end up divorcing like her parents did. But the day when she walked in on him with another woman in their bed—that's gross—she said that something snapped inside her and she knew she couldn't take it anymore."

He looks at me and says, "I don't blame her."

"Do y'know that the day she left, he went out and brought a woman home? I saw them and heard them too; it was gross. He doesn't care about anyone."

He shakes his head.

"I know, he's brought women home since you left. What are we going to do? I don't want to live with him anymore, I want to live with Mom."

"So do I."

Freddie says, "Well, there shouldn't be a problem with that, should there?"

"I don't know. She's with someone new...maybe he won't want us. I don't even know where they're living," I say, feeling suddenly hopeless.

"Have you met him?" Danny asks. "Who is he?"

I shake my head. "No, I haven't. I don't know if he brought her here yesterday; maybe she was scared that I'd be angry so she didn't bring him. His name's Donnie and she said that they work together, and he's wanted her to go out with him for years but she wouldn't because she didn't want to divorce Dad and make us suffer like she had as a child."

"She should have left him, because we suffered anyway," he says hotly.

"Yes, but not as much as she did." I can't believe that after all the hateful things I've ever said about my mother, I'm sticking up for her.

"Do y'know what else she told me? She told me that he killed my dog to make me hate her. You know how he blamed her for him doing it, well, she said that he's so spiteful inside that if I believed he killed Buster because he couldn't cope once she'd left, I would blame her and hate her. And she's right, I did hate her for it, even though none of it made any sense to me because *I* always took care of my dog, not Dad, and I couldn't see why he'd have to do it. She said that it was his way of hurting her, because it hurt me so much that I'd hate her forever and she'd have lost me forever."

"That's so sick," he says, and Freddie agrees.

"So he didn't care about hurting me, he just wanted to hurt Mom and didn't care who he hurt in the process," I say.

We can see him through the dining room window; he's standing up laughing with Tammy's mom.

Danny says, "I'd better go or he'll get mad."

"Will you be all right?"

I'm concerned for him and it feels new because I've never felt concerned for him before. I've always felt that he's been the lucky one, the one with the good looks and lots of friends. I know differently now; I know that even though he had those things he was still hurting inside, the same as me.

"It's hard to hold it all in," he says, "but it should be okay because he's too busy running around to notice what's going on inside me. If you hear from Mom again will you ask her if we can come and live with her? I'm going to go to her work and see if I can't catch her there. I'll call you and let you know what happens, okay?"

He stands up to go and gives me a hug awkwardly, and then he's gone. I don't go with him because I can't trust myself not to blast all my anger out at my dad, and I don't want Danny to have to ride home with Dad dumping *his* anger on him.

"Your brother's cool," Freddie says, "I like him. You look a lot alike."

"What? We're as different as can be," I say, my face screwed up.

"You may think so but I can see a lot of him in you, and you in him."

Rick comes out to the playground talking to someone I haven't seen before, and comes up to us.

"Hey, this is my cousin, Larry; he says he goes to your school, Mel."

The sun's in my eyes and I put my hand up to shade them so that I can see.

"I think we already met," he says, smiling at me.

I'm embarrassed, because beneath the shade of my hand I see that it's the nerd who sat next to me in class and picked up my pencil.

"You're cousins," I say foolishly, with my mouth open.

He nods. "Rick says that you're going to form a band; he says you can really sing."

"You should hear her," Freddie says.

I'm blushing, I know I am, partly because of what they're saying about me and I'm still not used to anyone saying nice things about me, but mainly because I pray he didn't see the disgust on my face when he picked up my pencil. His spots look less angry than that day and the one on his nose has obviously popped because it's not there anymore—like a beacon in the middle of his face. He's also been to the dentist because, as he smiles at me, I can't see his black tooth anymore.

"You're Danny's sister, aren't you? You look a lot alike."

"That's what I said," Freddie says, "but she won't listen."

I feel exasperated and change the subject.

"Rick says you play lead guitar. How long have you been playing?"

"Since I was big enough to hold a guitar," he says, "and I play every minute I can. It's all I do. I suffer school and go straight home to practice. I want to be as good as I can be."

"You should hear him play," Rick says, "Hang on, I'll go and get my guitar."

We sit on the bench and I feel a bit awkward. Larry knows I'm a nerd.

I know that he's heard all the nasty things people say about me at school, and as we sit here waiting for Rick to come back, I slip into a place where my newfound identity here at Beach Haven wavers. I'm scared that the little confidence that's grown within me will wither and die, and I'll be back in the front row at school, isolated along with the other nerds. I'm suddenly scared that I'll wake up in a minute with a teacher shouting at me to pay attention and all this will be an impossible dream. I desperately want to pinch myself.

Rick comes back and hands his guitar to Larry, and sits on the grass in front of him.

"Go on, play," Rick says.

He starts and my mouth drops open. His fingers are everywhere, and although the sun is beating down on me there are goose bumps all over my arms and I shiver. How could I ever have thought that he was a nerd?

Chapter Six

"**P**lay it again," Freddie says. "It's beautiful."

"What did I tell you?" Rick smiles with pride on his face. "Play some more."

"Go on," I say.

"Okay," and he loses himself in the sound his guitar is making.

I sit in awe and I know that if they really, seriously want me to sing with them, I'm going to do it. He plays even better than Rick does. My stomach turns with excitement.

"Are you serious about starting a band?" I venture to ask.

"Of course we are." Rick looks shocked that I could even ask, and I know that my self-doubt belittles me, so that I can't believe that he'd want me.

"I've been playing with a couple of kids from school," Larry says, "but they just think it's a bit of fun and don't show up for practice. I don't want to be around people like that. I want to be with people who share the same passion I have for music."

I was wrong when I first saw him and thought that he was a nerd with nothing to say; he's full and brimming over with passion for what he believes in. I've never heard anyone sound so animated about what they do, not even Danny, and he's crazy about skateboarding.

Rick looks at me hard and says, "Mel, you've got a fabulous voice, Larry's amazing, and I..." he grins, "...I do my best," trying to look coy. "Will you join our band?"

"I want to be in a band with people that are as dedicated as me," Larry says, "with people who want to be the very best they can be, and of course, people with talent."

My stomach's in a mess, churning and gurgling with nerves. Only two days ago I had the nerve to stand in front of a few safe people and sing in public for the first time. I can't believe that they want me. I know that I want to join them but I'm scared. What if I can't do it and I make a fool of myself? Neither of them has said anything about the way I look—I thought you had to have a perfect face and a perfect body to be in a band, and I've got neither. But then I look at Larry and think about his spots, and I don't feel so bad. There's no doubt in my mind that he's got everything it takes to be in a band, despite his spots; he's just made my body shiver with what he did with that guitar.

"What d'you think, Mel? We want you to join us," Rick says.

My face is flushed. Never in a month of Sundays would I ever have believed or dreamed that someone would want me for anything, let alone something as wonderful as being a singer in their band.

"I want to, but I'm scared."

"Don't you think we were too at first? But the more we practised, the better we got and the less scared we felt. As you get more confident it gives you the most amazing buzz."

"That's right. Once you start playing and get into it, it's like being in your own little world. It's amazing...I can't find the words to describe it."

Freddie digs me hard in the ribs.

"For heaven sake girl, I'd give anything to be in a band but I can't sing or play anything. I can't even dance without falling on my ass."

I giggle, remembering her jiving with Tammy.

"Okay," I say breathlessly, "I'll do it," and an excited sigh escapes me. I can't believe this is happening to me.

"Cool," Larry and Rick say together.

I feel so excited that I'm scared I'm going to throw up.

"Who else is going to be in it?" Freddie asks, "And where do you practice?"

"My mom and dad have a big house with a large yard and they turned the shed into a practice room for me...they had to soundproof it though, so that the neighbors won't complain." Rick grins.

I can just imagine what my dad would say if we were to practice in our house. I shake the thought away because I don't want to ruin this moment with thoughts of him.

Rick says, "One of my other cousins, Pete, is a great drummer and the bass player, Al, is my best friend. He's been there through everything."

I don't feel like I can ask what "everything" is. He suddenly looks sad.

A staff member comes out onto the playground and tells Larry that it's time for him to leave, so we all go in. Since it's not yet dinnertime I go to my room and lie down on my bed, dreaming.

I wonder about life, about choices and decisions, where they lead you. My thoughts take me to a place where reason is clouded by speculation. What if I didn't have such a rotten dad and my mom hadn't left? My dog would still be alive and I wouldn't have ended up here at Beach Haven. I would never have met Rick, Freddie or Miss Tina. Those awful things almost seem like they were the price I had to pay for meeting such wonderful people.

What if I'd been born to other parents, born pretty, but couldn't sing? I expect I'd have been able to sit in the back row in class and have the pick of any of the cool guys, but would I have ever experienced the excitement coursing through my body as it is now? It seems like life's a journey along a road with forks in it, and with each decision I make, I change the direction my life's heading.

I've never, ever thought about where my life's heading; it's been enough just to survive school and my home. I think about it now, though, as I nestle my head into my pillow to get comfortable. I know I can sing, so that'll be my future.

I think about the journey that has brought me to this point. If I hadn't reached rock bottom—the very lowest I could ever feel—I would never have come here and may never have had anyone point out to me that what I consider just a bathroom habit—singing in the shower—is actually beautiful.

As I lie here I realize that I've just acknowledged something about me as being "beautiful" and I go to reprimand myself but stop as sleep tugs at my senses.

The breeze is blowing the curtains into the room and I hear seagulls squawking far above me as I drift off, but as the sounds fade in the recesses of my mind, a figure walks slowly past me and sleep is snatched away.

I call out, shivering, and look around. I'm quite safe. I rest back into my pillows and think. I'm awake but part of my mind is still in that place where sleep and consciousness mingle, and gradually it dawns on me. I'm amazed at what the human brain can do; I know who the figure is that flits into my dreams. It's Larry.

Yesterday when I was with my mom in the dining room, Rick had loads of visitors, and they had left before my mom and me. I must have "seen" Larry as he walked past me but not recognized him, for I've only ever noticed him once and that was when I'd dropped my pencil in class. My brain must have filed it away somehow to come out in my dreams.

I'm fully awake and wonder about all the things that I know nothing about, and part of me longs to be older so that I can understand it all. As I muse upon my thoughts, I wonder how many other things I've "seen" but have not been aware of seeing. Do we just see what we want to see? I don't know, and my thoughts are chased away by Miss Tina coming down the hall telling us that it's time for dinner.

"You're so lucky," Tammy says, as Freddie tells her what happened this afternoon. "I'd give any- thing to be you."

I have no idea what to say. Until a few days ago I didn't even want to be me, so the thought of some- one else wanting to be me seems incredible; ugly old me with sunken piggy eyes, hooked nose and crooked teeth. I fill my mouth with food so that I can't answer her, and I listen—my face flushed—while she carries on about wishing she were me.

Rick joins us and he's so animated that he never

stops talking. I don't know how he manages to find time to eat his food but he does, between garbled inspirations about where we're going to go with this band.

"What're you going to call it?" Tammy asks.

I look at Rick with a question on my face and he frowns.

"Um, now, that's going to be a big deal. The name of a band's important. I don't know, got any suggestions?"

"Beach Haven Hoolies."

"No!" we all groan at once.

"Okay, okay, what about Haven Hoolies?"

"No!"

"How about Sweep Clean?"

Rick frowns for a moment, "Maybe, maybe, keep going."

"What about Pizza Parlor?"

"No!"

"How about Shoreline City?"

"Maybe, keep going."

I'm thinking really hard but don't really know where to start.

"Open Closet."

"No!"

"Open Book."

"Maybe."

I rack my brains; it has to mean something to me, to us, something special, something about succeeding and being the best. Something in my brain floats to the surface. I remember Danny pleading with Dad to buy him a new, top of the line skateboard for his birthday. Danny had said that he wanted to be the best skateboarder ever, and Dad had laughed, saying, "Never in a month of Sundays will you ever be the best skateboarder, or the best anything. Get real, kid."

I've thought about that statement over and over. What does it mean? A month of Sundays; it must mean a long, long time, or something that will never happen. There will never be a month of Sundays, so maybe it means that it's something rare...that's it, something rare.

I blurt out. "A Month of Sundays."

Rick looks at me with something in his face that's hard to describe.

"That's it. A Month of Sundays. That sounds great...A Month of Sundays. How'd you think of such a thing?"

"A month of Sundays means something really rare."

Rick says, "Well, your voice is rare and Larry's playing is rare, so it's a great name...I'll call Larry and the others later and see what they think."

We watch a movie and then it's time for bed, but I have trouble getting to sleep. My heart is bursting with love for Rick, and I toss and turn thinking about how he helped me when he saw me crying at visiting time. My mind is full of his smile.

So much has happened over the past three days that I feel like a different person. I see my mom differently, Danny differently, Larry differently and I'm starting to see myself differently, yet apart from myself, none of them has changed, it's just me that sees them differently. I drift off to sleep with these things floating about in my head.

• • • •

It's Monday and it's time for group. My nervousness isn't due to talking about painful things; I'm nervous to see Rick and be in the same room as him, and as Miss Tina starts talking I have a hard time staying focused on what she's saying.

"Today we're going to look at attitudes and what is called your Frame of Reference. I looked in my thesaurus to find out all the definitions of the word 'attitude,' and I found a lot."

She walks over to a flipchart and turns over a page to reveal lots of words.

"Perspective, stand, point of view, position, viewpoint, outlook, opinion, disposition, approach, manner, demeanor. All these words mean the same thing—attitude. Where does your attitude come from?"

She looks at us, waiting for someone to respond.

Freddie says, "From your parents."

"Yes, that's the biggest source, from your parents. And why's that?"

"Because they're with you the most when you're little," Julie says.

"Yes, and from birth to when you're six years old is the time when the foundations of your attitudes are laid down...how you feel about yourself and how you feel about others. After that age other people still influence your attitudes, especially your friends at school, but they build on those attitude foundations."

What friends? I think.

"Or if you have a bad experience at school, that can also influence your attitudes. Let's look at the kind of attitudes we have. What are your attitudes towards yourself, towards others and towards the world we live in?"

Miss Tina turns the sheet over on the flipchart and starts to draw what looks like a window with pretty curtains and then she draws the windowpanes, a cross in the middle of her picture.

"This is what I call your 'Window Pain of Reference'—it's how every one of us sees the world, and you each see it differently depending upon what your parents have encouraged you to see or not see. You can be in any one of these windowpanes, and if you're in that particular pane, the way you see everything in this world will be influenced by your attitudes—attitudes instilled in you by the people who brought you up. Each pane of the 'Window Pain of Reference' reflects the way in which you see yourself and how you see others."

She starts to write with a red marker in each windowpane. In the first one she writes, "I'm OK and you're OK too," then turns to us and says, "This is where every human being *should* be; he respects himself and others. He sees himself as being 'okay' and others as being 'okay,' too. This is the only position or windowpane where you are unlikely to feel emotional pain. If you find yourself in any of the other three positions, or windowpanes, you will feel pain; hence the reason why I call it the 'Window Pain of Reference.'"

She then writes in the next windowpane, "I'm OK but you're not OK," and then she looks more serious. "This and the next two windowpanes are not good; none of us needs to be seeing life from these perspectives."

Several of us shift in our seats. She points to the second windowpane.

"This windowpane in our 'Window Pain of Reference' shows that we see ourselves as better than other people, and although we may strive to be better than the next person in many ways, (money, education, clothes, cars) what we really crave is for others to like us. But because this person sees others as being 'not okay,' any praise or friendship from people they think are worthless is worthless to them, and so they remain empty, and their belief that other people are 'not okay' is confirmed."

In the next windowpane she writes, "I'm not OK but you're OK."

"If you view life from this position, your self-esteem will be very low and you'll filter out anything nice that anyone says to you. It also means that you'll try really hard to please other people and will probably end up doing things that will hurt you."

I'm sure my face is red because I feel really hot. That's me; she's just described me. I know I'm "not okay" but I saw those boys as being "okay," and they used me, they hurt me.

In the last windowpane she writes "I'm not OK and you're not OK either."

"This last windowpane in the 'Window Pain of Reference' is the worst position of all—it's where every human being's despair comes from. Anyone who sees life from this perspective would see themselves as being "not okay" and everyone else as being "not okay" either, so no matter what they do, they'll rubbish it, and any praise they get they'll ignore or filter it out of their minds."

I don't think I'm in that windowpane. I think other people are "okay," but I don't think I'm "okay."

"While you're here, we need to get you into this windowpane." She points to the windowpane that says, "I'm OK and you're OK, too."

"This is where we should all be; respecting ourselves as being valuable and respecting other people as being valuable, too."

I so want to be in that windowpane but I don't know how to get there, and I pray that she's going to show me how. I can see exactly what she's saying and it feels like someone has just opened the curtains so that I can see properly for the first time in my life. I respect other people but I don't respect myself. I hate it. I want to respect myself but I don't know how to. I pray that she'll show me because I really don't know what to do to get into the healthy, good windowpane, but I want to so badly.

I can see why Miss Tina calls it a "Window Pain of Reference" because *I* feel pain when I recognize that I see myself as being "not okay." It hurts, but I also feel a twinge of anger, too.

Why do I feel as if I'm "not okay"? Did my parents not praise me enough? I know that my dad has belittled me all my life, and my mom didn't help me know that I was special, or even just "okay." I know she said that she didn't want to be divorced because her parents had and she'd been hurt, but as I'm sitting here trying to cope with my feelings of being "not okay," I wish things had been different. I don't blame her but I feel sad that it's me that has to deal with the leftovers of her and dad's mistakes, especially when coping with it is extra hard *because* I feel so "not okay."

"It can be tough learning to believe in yourself when all your life you've felt as if you're 'not okay,'" Miss Tina says, "and it takes practice to allow yourself to actually *hear* any praise that may be given to you. Self-esteem is like a delicate flower that needs to be nurtured and watered, little and often, until it grows strong and is able to stay strong in a storm... when life gets tough and the beliefs you have about yourself may be challenged."

I think I actually heard the praise everyone gave me after Show Night because I *do* feel a bit better about myself than when I first came here.

"It can be tough learning to see other people as being "okay," too, especially if your only experiences with others have told you that they're not to be trusted, or that they will hurt you. You will filter out any good that they may have in them and focus only on the bad so that it fits in with your perception of other people being 'not okay.' Human beings have the ability to filter out information, which will challenge how we see ourselves and others, and it helps to keep us *stuck* in the same place, with low self-esteem. We need to get rid of this 'filter' so that we can challenge and change our attitudes."

I think I know what she means because both Larry and Freddie said that I look a lot like Danny; if they can both see it, surely it must be true. Yet because I see myself as ugly and him as good-looking, I must have been filtering out anything that would make me challenge my belief. Freddie said my brother's cool, yet until yesterday I couldn't see it.

Miss Tina's right, each person's perspective is different from someone else's, and as I stop filtering new information about people I start to see them differently. I see my mom differently, Danny differently, Larry differently, and I'm starting to see myself differently, yet apart from myself, none of them has changed, it's just me that sees them differently.

"I have another story for you," Miss Tina grins, "to try and help you understand the 'Window Pain of Reference,' how from birth our attitudes are molded, by our parents initially, and then by society. Then depending upon whether those attitudes are good or bad, we will see life from that perspective, and what we see may not be what's really there at all. It's called 'The Filter Goggles.'"

Oh, good, I love stories.

"Are you ready?" she grins again, and I swear she's enjoying herself.

• • • •

Far, far away in the land that bobbed in and out of view depending upon the sea mist, between two rugged mountains nestled a beautiful village above a vast lake that glistened and shone in the sunlight. It was the most beautiful place on earth, but legend told the villagers that hundreds of years ago a terrible plague had come upon the people who lived in the village.

The plague attacked their eyes and their ability

to see any beauty in themselves, or in other people, or to be able to see the beauty that surrounded them. So in order to protect themselves, the village elders of that time proclaimed that every person should wear a pair of goggles so that the plague would be filtered from their eyes and it would not blind them.

The people became very angry at being told what to do, so to appease them the elders said that they wouldn't dictate what type of goggles they should wear. They could learn how to make them so that their goggles were uniquely theirs, and they would be happy to wear them. But many people believed that they knew best, so few attended the goggle-making classes.

As soon as a baby was born he wore the goggles his mother and father had made, which were exactly the same as theirs, but were different from every other family's goggles. As the child grew, he saw the village in exactly the same way his parents did, but because some of the goggles were made by people who had refused to take lessons, some were flawed. Although they filtered the plague and prevented it from getting in their eyes, those goggles distorted their vision so that they weren't able to gaze on the beauty around them.

Each family's goggles were different depending upon the amount of care the parents had taken to make them. Those who had learned made good, sturdy goggles without any flaws, and their children were able to see beauty in themselves, beauty in each other and the beauty all around them.

Other families who refused to learn from the elders made goggles that were flawed, and their children saw a distorted view of themselves, others and the village. Some saw beauty in themselves but not in others, and others saw beauty in others but not in themselves, and all were blinded to the beauty around them.

Other families made goggles that were so flawed that their children's vision was totally distorted, and they saw no beauty in themselves, no beauty in others, and no beauty all around them.

And so it was throughout each generation of villagers—no one questioned the coming of the plague or sought to rid the village of it; it was just the way it was.

There was much fighting among the villagers, who all saw themselves and others differently, and the elders, who were dismayed, moved further up the mountains so that they could no longer hear the people arguing.

As two elders sat one evening in the shade of the sinking sun, they gradually noticed that the air was clear and sweet, and one elderly, white-haired grandfather with a long white beard sniffed the air knowingly.

"You know," he said, "there's something wrong

with the way we live this life. For generations we have done as those before us have done and never questioned anything or tried to learn new ways. Why have we merely accepted our ancestors' beliefs and attitudes and not seen for ourselves? We have never tried to rid ourselves of the plague that has threatened to blind our people. Why?"

He tugged at his goggles.

His friend peered at him through his own goggles, thinking that the old man had taken leave of his senses as he pulled his goggles from his face.

Both men gasped, one with fear and the other with wonder. There was no plague waiting to smite them down or blind them. The air was sweet and clear, just as the elder had suspected.

"Hurry, hurry," he said, rubbing his eyes. "Take your goggles off. Look see! There is no plague and we have no need to filter our vision or to protect our eyes. We can see, really see."

His friend pulled his goggles off at once and couldn't believe his eyes. Both men feasted on the beauty before them, the rugged snow-tipped mountains, a deer that nibbled lazily at a bush, rabbits that hopped freely at its feet, and the eagles soaring high above them. Tears flowed down both men's faces, for all their lives they had lived constrained by their own parents' goggles, and it was only now that they saw the beauty that had been there all the time.

They ran to find their friends—who thought they

were sick and had lost their minds—until they, too, ripped their goggles off, and saturated themselves in the wonders before them.

Far away, where the cries of the villagers were lost on the wind, was the vast expanse of shimmering water, the lake that they didn't know was there, yet it had been there all the time.

"We have to go back down to the village and tell everyone that the plague is no longer here," an elder said urgently, and then his face turned to sadness, "...and I wonder if it ever was there."

They packed up their things at once and made their way down the trail towards the village, and as they got closer, they heard the villagers arguing about who was better than the next, who was prettier than the next and who was the most wealthy. Those whose goggles were so distorted that they saw no beauty in themselves or others lay slumped in the gutter, drunk on cheap wine, or else they were racing around the village not knowing what they were doing, stealing and selling potent weeds that grew in the fields.

As the elders walked into the village, tired and weary, but exhilarated and driven to impart their message, the villagers peered through their goggles and were horrified.

"Take them off, take them off," the elders all cried, but the villagers refused.

"Don't listen to them, for they're old and crazy.

Don't take them off or the plague will get you and you'll all be blinded."

But one by one the children, who had missed the elders, took off their goggles and stood dumbstruck as they gazed at the sights around them. Mothers, horrified that their children might suddenly be blinded or struck down, ran to put the goggles back on their children's faces, but they couldn't catch them, for when they saw their intention, the children ran towards the great shimmering lake. The mothers screamed, for their children had disappeared. They couldn't see the lake and all its beauty, so in desperation they ripped the goggles from their faces and immediately they saw their children and ran after them.

It was only after they caught up with them that they began to notice the beauty around them, and when they did so, they wept in awe. They held their children's hands and together they stared at the lake, the birds that flew across it or bobbed on its shimmering surface, and the fish that leapt from the water. They turned around and saw the rugged mountains; snow settled over the peaks and the trees lining the slopes, where the creatures played, free from fear. Then they looked at each other and were overwhelmed by what they saw. Those who thought they were better than the others around them saw the beauty in others, and those who had not been able to see their own beauty saw it for the *first time. They wept and were finally free.*

They walked back to the village, hand in hand, their souls shining through their bright clear eyes, and walked up to the elders and hugged them. Their men stood watching anxiously, still wearing their goggles. One by one they took them off, and gasps of joy escaped their lips. Those who had thought that others were better than themselves now saw themselves as being just as beautiful, and those who only acknowledged their own beauty saw their beauty reflected in others.

A great hush and stillness came over the village as everyone looked in wonder at each other and around them, their anger and arguments silenced, for they had no need to persecute or defend themselves anymore; they were equally as beautiful.

One by one each person went to help those who were slumped in the gutter, drunk on cheap wine.

"Take your goggles off," but they held on to them tightly, afraid, lest someone see straight into their hearts, which they believed were worthless and shriveled.

"Take them off," a kindly elder said gently. "It's okay. Look at us, we're okay, and you will be, too."

The elders had to help those poor villagers whose goggles were so flawed that everything they saw through them was distorted; they were fearful and trembling, but as their goggles were gently lifted away from their faces, they wept and were finally free. They saw their own beauty, and the beauty in others. The elders helped them to their feet and, as they stared around them, their mouths gaped open in disbelief at the beauty they had missed all their lives.

Not all the people believed the elders, though, and there were still some villagers who refused to take their goggles off. Some were scared to change, or do things differently from the way the ancestors had for hundreds of years, and others were just stubborn and refused to change. They continued to fail to see beauty in themselves, or in others, and were completely unaware of the beauty around them.

And so it was throughout time; those who still wore their goggles forced their children to wear the same, and they grew to be just like their parents— some saw no beauty in themselves, some saw no beauty in others, and those who had the most distorted goggles saw no beauty at all.

● ● ● ●

Miss Tina looks up at us and smiles; I have tears in my eyes.

Chapter Seven

"Do you all understand what it means?" Miss Tina asks. "I wanted to call the goggles, 'Attitude Goggles,' for that's what they were. The villagers wore 'attitude goggles' that blinded them to what life was really like. Depending upon their attitudes, they filtered out everything that didn't fit in with their perception of life, a way of thinking that was virtually forced upon them by their parents. It's likely that whichever windowpane in the 'Window Pain of Reference' your parents view their world from, it will have some effect upon you and how you see your world.

"Y'know, whether we have high self-esteem or low self-esteem depends on how our families treated us throughout our childhood. Some parents are better parents than others, depending upon how they were brought up themselves. Unless you have been abused, or live with very abusive parents, which is unforgivable, there is no place for any blame towards your parents, because for the most part they were just doing the best they could with what they'd been shown by their own parents. So I don't want any of you to think that blaming your parents for the problems you have in life is all right; it's not. It's okay to feel blame if they have sexually or physically abused you; that's different. But if they have just made poor decisions that have hurt your self-esteem, then what you need to do is to learn to understand, not blame. It's a very different feeling. Can I use you as an example, Melody?"

I nod, feeling apprehensive, wondering what she's going to say.

"Melody's mother was so intent on not making the same mistakes her parents had, that she made other ones instead, which ultimately hurt Melody as much as she herself had been hurt as a child. But it wasn't her intention to hurt her, she just made poor decisions. Yet it seems as if Melody's dad, by killing her dog, willfully set out to hurt her, and that's abusive behavior."

I swallow hard.

"Which windowpane do you think he sees his world through?" she asks me.

"Um." I think for a moment...my head's spinning. "He's 'okay' and others aren't."

"It could be," she says, frowning as she thinks,

"but it could also be the windowpane that says, 'I'm not OK and you're not OK either.'"

"How come?"

"Because deep down, I wouldn't mind betting that he's a very unhappy man inside. Why would you do something that will make other people hate you? Sooner or later when he can't hide what's really inside him, everyone will leave and he'll be all alone."

I nod. I don't care much about him, though, whether he sees himself as "okay" or "not okay," because what's obvious to me is that he sees everyone else as being "not okay," including me and Danny.

"Which windowpane do you think your mom sees her world through?" Miss Tina asks.

"Well, I think she sees me and Danny as being 'okay,' but I don't think she sees herself as being 'okay,' otherwise why would she let Dad hurt her so much?"

"You're right, it sounds like her own self-esteem is low, which wouldn't be surprising, given that she'd had a hard time herself as a child. She's like one of the women in the story who wore her 'attitude goggles,' which told her that she was 'not okay' and other people were. She believed it until she was forced to take the goggles off and learn a new way."

"What d'you think the elders felt when they had the courage to take their goggles off and learned that for all that time, their whole lives, they had lived under the impression that the world was one way when it was actually another way?"

"Cheated," Rick said.

"Sad," Tammy says.

"Both, I imagine," says Miss Tina. "I think it's wonderful that they finally took them off, even though it was late in their lives; that means there's still hope for everyone no matter how old they are. They can change their attitudes, no matter how late it may seem. But how sad that they didn't get to take them off earlier in their lives, so that they could be rid of attitudes that stopped them from learning new ways or feeling good about themselves and others. How sad that they wasted all that time being one way when they could have been another, more healthy way."

I think of my dad, although I don't want to, and I wonder whether he'll ever take off his "attitude goggles"; I doubt it.

"This is one of the reasons I love working with young people. You are like the children in the story. You have the courage to take off your 'attitude goggles' and see life in a healthier way. Even if your self-esteem is low at the moment, you have the time to nurture it, so that even when things go wrong in life, which they will at times, your self-esteem will still remain high, and you'll be able to see the beauty in yourselves, others and the world."

"How do you make your self-esteem grow?" I dare to ask.

Miss Tina smiles at me. "It doesn't happen over-night. It's a gradual process that starts by recognizing which 'Window Pain of Reference' you view your world from, then being determined to get into the 'I'm OK and you're OK too,' windowpane. The way to do that is to identify each time you filter out something nice that someone says to you, and then force yourself to *hear* what they say about you and *accept* it."

She smiles at us. "It's a little bit like being a gardener caring for a delicate 'self-esteem flower'; you have to water it gently and often to make it grow."

She stands up and walks back to the flipchart.

"Melody, before you sang on Show Night, you didn't seem to be able to *hear* anything nice that anyone said to you, is that right?"

I nod.

"But after you sang, everyone told you how beau-tiful your voice is, and with so many people saying it, you had to accept that it was true. It was then that you *heard* it. Is that right?"

I nod again.

"And did that make you feel better about your-self?"

"Lots."

She turns the page over on the flipchart and starts to draw.

"Okay, so Melody started to feel a little bit better after hearing something different from what she's heard, or felt, in the past about herself. But for your self-esteem to really grow you need to hear good things about yourself over and over, so that your self-esteem not only *grows* but it *strengthens*. If you only hear one good thing about yourself, then your 'attitude goggles' will tell you that 'it was a fluke,' or 'people were only being nice because they had to be,' and you'll disappear back into that place where low self-esteem lives...and it's cold, dark and barren there."

We look at what she's been drawing while she's been talking to us. It looks like a tree in winter with no leaves on it.

"How about we look at it like this. Every fall the trees shed their leaves and the trees end up like this—cold, barren and bare. Let's imagine that this tree represents low self-esteem...it's cold, barren and bare, and cannot bear any fruit. The tree in the summer, though, is covered in leaves and may fruit. Let's imagine that a tree covered in leaves represents high self-esteem. Now, to get from low self-esteem to high self-esteem let's imagine that every leaf is what we call an 'affirmation,' something that someone says is good about you."

She grins at me. "Come here, baby," she says, and I get up with butterflies in my stomach wondering what she's going to do.

"Stand here; you are my Self-Esteem Tree."

She pulls my arms out and I try not to giggle.

"This poor tree has no leaves," she says, feigning sadness, and dabs her eyes with a tissue. "We need to give her some leaves so that she won't be cold, barren and bare."

She walks around the circle of kids and gives each one a pencil and a piece of paper that's shaped like a leaf.

"Write your affirmations about Melody on your leaf. Write on the leaf something good that you see in her, and I've written 'singing,' so choose something different; then when you've done that, come and tape it back onto her poor, bare tree."

She walks over to me and tapes a leaf to my sleeve that says, "Melody has a heavenly voice," written on it.

"Keep those branches up," she says, as my arms begin to droop, and we laugh. I love her; she makes my heart smile. I've never known how to play before, but she shows me. I'm a tree!!

Rick comes over and tapes his leaf on me, and says, "I think you have amazing strength and courage."

I blush and feel an overwhelming sense of love for him.

Freddie comes next and her leaf says, "Melody has a sense of adventure."

Tammy's says, "Melody is full of warmth and is a good friend who listens."

Paul's leaf says, "Melody is brave."

Everyone else comes over and tapes their leaves on

me, and my arms are about to drop off, they're aching so badly, but my heart is bursting with happiness.

"Okay, hush now," Miss Tina says, because we're all making so much noise. "Now, look at our beautiful tree; you can put your arms down now, sweetheart," and I let out a groan, but I'm too scared to shake the cramp out of my arms in case I shake all my leaves off and end up being cold, barren and bare again.

"Our beautiful tree is covered in leaves that give her affirmations about herself, and as each leaf sticks firmly to her, so her self-esteem grows and is strengthened. If Melody has a bad day and someone says something nasty to her that hurts her and makes a leaf fall off, she will still retain her strong sense of high self-esteem. This is because she has lots and lots of 'affirmation leaves' to remind her that she's valuable and worthy, and they help to strengthen her high self-esteem. But think, if no one ever praised her or told her that she was valuable and worthy, she'd be cold, barren and bare. That's terrible, and she'd have very low self-esteem. If someone said something nice to her and put an affirmation leaf on her Self-Esteem Tree, she'd feel a little better about herself, but then if someone was nasty to her and the leaf fell off, she'd go back to being cold, barren and bare again. She wouldn't have enough 'affirmation leaves' on her tree to help her cope with losing one. Can you see what I mean?"

I think so.

"So raising your self-esteem takes some time and you need support. Self doubt can make your 'affirmation leaves' fall off too, so you need to be told over and over that you are valuable and worthy."

A boy speaks out, "Yeah, but my parents never say anything good about me, and they'd laugh in my face if I asked them to say something nice about me."

"That's very sad. All parents should say nice things about their children, but I realize that if often doesn't happen. This presents you with a challenge. You have to find the strength inside you to give yourself 'affirmation leaves,' you have to remember everything you've learned here at Beach Haven and quietly remind yourself that you are valuable and worthy. I'm not saying it's easy, but for some of you that's going to be the only way to make sure that there are 'affirmation leaves' on your Self-Esteem Tree.

"When you leave here, if someone is nasty to you and one of your 'affirmation leaves' falls off, call us and we'll give you another to stick back on, so that you can still build your self-esteem and be covered in wonderful leaves and you'll 'bear fruit.' Beach Haven will always be here for all of you, always. You need never feel that you're alone again. Pick up the phone and you'll be with us again, long enough to make sure all your 'affirmation leaves' are firmly stuck to your Self-Esteem Tree."

She laughs. "Okay, you trees, we're finished for today. You did a good job."

Freddie comes over to me and helps me retrieve all my wonderful "affirmation leaves" and I put them into an envelope; they are a gift, and I've never had such a wonderful gift before.

"Hey, you make a great tree," Freddie nudges me and I giggle.

After lunch Miss Tina calls to me as we're about to go outside.

"Come here a minute, Melody."

She takes me into the staff room and tells me to sit down.

"Your mother's been on the phone. Apparently Danny met her at work and begged her to let you both come and live with her."

"What did she say?"

"She said, 'Yes.'"

My heart leaps; I can't believe it, I don't have to go home and live in the same house as that man ever again. In fact, I never have to see him again. A strange sense of stillness comes over me and I feel a little sick.

"I spoke to your mom earlier and she sounds really positive, well, more than that, really. She was so excited that I think you and Danny have just made her day. I think she's really beaten herself up about leaving you both, and particularly after what happened to your poor dog. I don't think she could believe that you both wanted to live with her."

"Any day," I say. "I never want to see my dad

again after what he's done."

"Be still, sweetheart, remember...'There's no blame; only understanding.'"

I don't listen; he killed my dog for no other reason than to hurt my mom and me. Somewhere deep inside me, I may be able to understand that he sees life through the "I'm not OK and you're not OK either" windowpane; but that doesn't help how I'm feeling right now. I blame him and I never want to see him again.

She brushes my hand with hers. "What will be, will be; just let it be, and it'll come right in the end."

"What about Mom's new man? Does he want us to live with him?" It dawns on me that I don't know where they live. "Where do they live?"

"They live in your home town, and Donnie wants both of you to live with them. I spoke to him today and he seems nice. Give him a chance, Mel."

"Anybody's got to be better than Dad," I say, knowing that I sound spiteful, but I can't help it.

"He's a musician...I think you'll like him."

"What does he play?"

"The piano, I think, and he writes songs."

Suddenly I feel excited. What if he were to write songs for our band?

She breaks into my thoughts. "So that means that you can go home tomorrow."

I feel faint. Rick, I can't leave Rick. Tears spring

into my eyes. I feel sick. I'm really happy that my mom wants us to live with her but I'm overcome with panic. I've gotten used to seeing Rick everyday, as soon as I get up, at breakfast, group, class, lunch, group and class again, then sitting on the beach talking and playing guitar. I can't go home.

She leans forward and looks into my eyes; I look away, wiping the tears as they spill down my face.

"Beautiful girl, you'll be all right, you will. You have such talent. You are truly beautiful."

I brush her away. No, I'm not. I don't want to go. Being at Beach Haven has been the best thing that's ever happened to me, and even though I know life with Mom and her new man will be better than living with Dad, it won't be as good as being here with Miss Tina and all my new friends. I know a sob escapes me as I think of Rick.

"Rick tells me that you are going to be the singer in his new band. That's wonderful, it really is. He's leaving the day after tomorrow, too, and Freddie's going on Friday. No more jiving," she says, and I laugh through the sobs that still escape me.

My head's spinning and I try to tell myself that Rick and Freddie won't even be here, so there's no reason to cry, in fact it would be worse staying here if they'd gone. But that's not entirely true, because it isn't only Rick and Freddie that make it wonderful here; it's Miss Tina and the others as well.

"Listen, I keep saying it, and I want you to hear it

again and again. Beach Haven is your second home, and we are your second family. We are always here, and when things get tough, you get on the phone and call us, okay?

"D'you know why I love the beach so much? It's because it changes every day yet it's still the same underneath. Every day the waves bring something different to the shore—bottles, flotsam, old boots, coins...treasure. That's like life. Every day something new will land on your shore, something precious. Remember what the villagers saw when they took their goggles off—they saw things that they'd never noticed before."

She takes my hands.

"It's exciting, Melly. *(She called me my baby name. How did she know?)* Life is exciting, even though it hurts sometimes. But from now on, no matter what happens at home, whether it's good or bad, you have a second home, Beach Haven, and we'll always be here for you. Call us anytime you need us, or even when you don't need us, and we'll be here for you."

I'm crying, softly though, and it feels okay. I've never known anyone so supportive or nurturing, and somewhere in my mind I see her pouring water from a watering can onto my delicate self-esteem flower, watching and waiting for me to grow. My tears are part of that growth and she makes it okay.

I go back to my room and cry some more, not trusting myself to join the kids outside. But not wanting to waste what little time I have left being alone in my room, I splash my face with cold water and head outside.

Freddie takes one look at me and says, "What's going on? Why are you crying?"

What little strength I thought I had leaves me like a traitor, and I cry some more on her shoulder but manage to blurt out that I have to leave.

"Sugar, we all have to leave. I'm going in a couple of days, but that doesn't mean it's over. We're friends, and friends remain friends wherever they are and whatever they're doing. Hey, d'you think you're going to get rid of me that quickly? No way. I'm going to be your makeup artist and your beautician."

I cry even harder; my tears flow from gratitude and relief. I may have to leave, but I'm only leaving the building. Everyone that means something to me is coming with me, either in body or in spirit, or on the end of a phone.

"C'mon," she says, handing me a screwed up tissue. "Let's walk along the shore...I can smell my feet from here."

She makes me giggle; I love her so much. My mom would never let me be friends with her if I brought her home from school because she can be what Mom calls loud. Yet meeting her in this place has shown me what's inside her heart, and she sees what's inside mine, and it's what's inside that matters. I'd never have known her if we'd met at school. I feel so lucky.

We scrunch our way over the loose sand and wade in the ocean up to our knees. The water's warm and clear.

We spend the afternoon "resting and growing," wandering up and down the shore searching for shells. I want to take some home with me to remind myself of this day, messing about on the beach with my best friend.

At dinner I look around me and feel sad that this is the last evening I'll sit here surrounded by all these kids. I feel a huge lump in my throat and, as my eyes brim with tears again, I silently curse myself.

I can't eat and I push my plate away uneaten, for there's a knot in my stomach preventing me from eating; it's huge, twisted, and raw. Freddie scrapes her plate clean and goes off to get a piece of pie. She looks at me as she sits down and grins. I can't help laughing. She's so funny. She stuffs pie into her mouth and looks as if she's in ecstasy, murmuring "mmmmm" as Tammy and I watch her. Then she chases the crumbs around her plate and finally lays her fork down with a determined look of satisfaction. We laugh and wait for a belch, but it doesn't come. She just sits up and stares us straight in the eye and says, "What?" which makes us crack up laughing again.

I drink water, figuring that it will replace some of the tears I've cried. It's been so strange because I've cried with fear and I've cried with sadness, but I've also cried with joy. I don't seem to know where I'm at.

Everyone leaves the dining room except Freddie and me...it's our turn to clean up.

"Y'know, Mel, it really doesn't matter that we won't be here at Beach Haven, because we'll still be together," Freddie says, when she notices that I've become quiet. "Listen, I told you, didn't I? I'm your makeup artist and beautician, so you won't be able to get rid of me."

She laughs and hugs me, and I hug her back, hard.

We clean up and turn the lights off, and as we walk up the hall I can see Rick outside on the swings.

"Go and talk to him," Freddie says.

She walks off and I push the door open, feeling the night breeze blowing on my face.

"Hey," I say, not knowing what else to say.

"You finished cleaning up?"

"Yep."

I sit on the swing next to him and we sway as we did two days ago. There's something comforting about swaying on swings, something I can't fathom.

"So you're leaving tomorrow?" he says.

"Yes." I don't dare say anything else because I don't trust myself.

"I leave the next day," he says. "Y'know, kids come and go here, some stay a day, others stay weeks or months. Nothing lasts forever; everything changes. I guess that's life. It's scary though."

I find the courage to speak. "I'm scared. I'm scared to go home because home isn't there anymore; I'm going to a new home and I don't know how that'll be. I'm scared to death to go back to school...I don't know if I can face it. But most of all I'm scared to say goodbye to Beach Haven and everyone here."

"I know," he says, "I have to go home but I'm not ready. I don't think I'll ever be ready. I don't want to go. This is such a wonderful place that everything by comparison is empty, nothing, a bit like Miss Tina's winter tree with no leaves on it."

A flicker of fun flashes across his solemn face. "Hey, you make a great tree."

"Thanks."

"You're welcome."

We're both quiet. I don't know what to say and I realize that I don't even know why Rick's here. I've been so busy with my own issues that I haven't even bothered with his. I feel ashamed but quickly remember my Self-Esteem Tree; I just stripped a leaf off myself.

"My parents wanted me to go home a month ago but I couldn't face it."

I feel like an intruder. I don't know what to say but I'm dying to ask him. I have no idea why he's here; in fact, when I first got here I thought he was a member of staff because he seemed so "together." I don't know how to ask him so we sit in silence for a while and listen to the waves roll up the beach beyond the playground.

"D'you want to walk?" he asks.

"Yeah, okay."

We walk down onto the beach, the moon shining across the water. We sit on the sand, just yards away from the playground because it's dark and we know that we'll have to go in soon.

He's crying. I don't know what to do.

I put my hand on his back awkwardly, wanting to hold him but not knowing how to go about it. I can feel his body shaking and shuddering beneath my hand.

He rides it out in the same way I did when my dog was dead, and suddenly it comes to an abrupt halt. He turns his head and looks me straight in the eye.

"Melly, you're so beautiful, so special."

I lose my breath...he's going to kiss me, I know it, and I brace myself, praying that I do it right.

But his lips are nowhere near mine. He reaches out for me and hugs me as if his life depended upon it. And while I'm ready for him to kiss me, my first real kiss, my first *proper* kiss, I chase the memory of those two boys away...they don't exist. I can feel his body trembling against mine.

Chapter Eight

I don't know what to think. He's holding me tightly but doesn't make any attempt to kiss me. Have I done something wrong? I don't know what to do, so I just hold him back.

Slowly his shoulders stop shaking and his breathing slows.

"What's the matter?" I ask him carefully.

He shakes his head.

"I'm sorry, Mel, I'm sorry. I didn't mean to dump all that on you, but sometimes it's just so hard to keep it in."

"What's wrong?"

"It's Jenny; she's gone. Sometimes it's so hard."

I don't know what to say, so I don't say anything. I feel ashamed of myself because I'm glad his girlfriend's gone because now he can be mine, all mine. If I can get over the pain I felt at what those two boys did to me, then he can get over his ex-girlfriend. I'll make him feel better, and he'll soon forget all about her.

We hear a whistle and that means the staff are calling us back in.

I brush the sand off me, and we walk back towards the door, but even though he's just held me, he doesn't hold my hand.

We join the others who are drinking milk and eating cookies, and as we go off to bed, Rick looks at me and says, "Thanks, Mel."

What for? I don't know what he means.

I lie in my bed with a wonderful, warm glow flowing through me. I love him so much; being in his arms was heavenly. Even though we're both leaving here, he'll still be with me. I toss and turn trying to remind myself to swap phone numbers, and as thoughts of "what if I forget or he forgets, I may never see him again" curdle my stomach, I jump out of bed and tie a knot in my sock to remind me first thing in the morning to swap phone numbers.

Sleep still evades me as my mind races with worries. What's it going to be like living with Mom's new man? I hope he likes me...I hope I like him. What's it going to be like going back to school? I feel really sick when thoughts of school pop into my head. I don't think I can face it – the images of those two boys and their friends laughing at me, and all the pretty girls from the back row jeering at me. I toss and turn until my sheets are in a tangle.

I don't feel any better in the morning because it's now only a few hours before I have to leave. My stomach's sick, my heart hurts, and I'm scared out of my mind.

As soon as I see Miss Tina I ask her for my mom's phone number and make copies to give to Rick and Freddie. They both give me their numbers and I feel a little easier inside.

The morning drags as we sit through class and we have to write an essay entitled, "What scares me the most."

It's quite easy to write because what scares me the most is going back to school and facing all the bullies again, so I know what to write. I think about my Self-Esteem Tree and wonder if I have enough "affirmation leaves" to cope with losing one every time someone says something nasty to me.

My stomach is so twisted as I write that I have to go to the bathroom, but I return to my desk feeling no better. I write about being a tree in the school playground and how it feels to be cold, barren and bare and then about how I'm going to try to cope with it. I'm going to make sure that I have money for the phone on me all the time. Then if it gets too bad and all my leaves fall off, I can call Beach Haven and ask for an "affirmation leaf" so that my tree won't be naked and vulnerable.

The teacher makes us read aloud what we've written and I'm quite pleased with mine. She says that I have good problem solving skills, and says that it'll be a good way of coping with feeling alone and isolated, even if no one bullies me. They will, I know they will, and when I say so, she says that my way of coping will really help because while I'm on the phone talking to people who really like me and care about me, I'll be smiling and laughing. She says that it's hard for bullies to carry on bullying when they see their victim laughing and having a good time and not reacting to the horrid things they are saying. She tells me that they'll soon get tired of it and move on to someone else if I don't react in the way they want me to.

"It would be even better if you had a cell phone," Freddie says, "because then you could pull it out and use it wherever you are, and not have to try and find the nearest public phone."

"Yes, that's a good point," the teacher says. "Will that be possible, Melody?"

"I doubt it; it costs money."

"Well, talk it over with your mother and see what she says."

I decide that I'm going to ask Miss Tina to ask Mom for me, and also to ask her to let me wear makeup like all the other girls, so I'll feel better about the way I look. If *I* ask her she may just turn around and say no without realizing what it means to me, or how important it is.

After break we have group with Miss Tina. I feel

a bit sad because this will be the last group I have with her, and I say so when she asks if anyone has got anything to say before she starts.

"Melody, have you forgotten that I go to your school once a week to hold a group? You can come to that if you want to."

Suddenly I feel so much better and school doesn't seem quite so frightening.

Miss Tina starts to talk.

"As Melody is leaving us this afternoon I wanted to do something special for her, something that focuses on the issues she's worked on while she's been here. When you first got here, Melody, you constantly said that you were ugly and talked all the time about other people being more beautiful or pretty than you. No matter how many times all of us told you that you were not ugly, you didn't seem to be able to hear it. I'm so proud of you because you've worked really hard to see yourself in a different way."

I'm shifting about in my seat, wondering what she's going to say next.

"Well, you made me do a lot of thinking. We all know the sayings, 'Beauty is in the eye of the beholder' and 'Beauty is only skin deep.' Well, I sat and thought about it. What *does* make a person attractive? What is it? Shall we go around the room and say what each of you thinks is attractive to the opposite sex?"

Freddie says, "A sense of humor."

Paul says, "Being smart."

Tammy says, "Being thin."

Julie says, "Being a good dancer."

Rick says, "Being faithful and a good listener."

"Being handsome."

"Having money."

"Being sensitive."

"Being good at sports."

"Telling jokes."

"Being romantic."

"Being pretty."

"Okay, stop," Miss Tina says. "Can you see that no one thing is attractive to everyone, and only two of you referred to physical features? Most of you thought of other qualities that are attractive, which have very little to do with the way you look. When I was thinking about what it is that makes us attractive, I came to the conclusion that it's about how much a person shines and sparkles; whether they've got their *lights* on or not, whether they've got a zest for living or not. Attractiveness comes from having your lights on, and not from physical features.

"So I've written a special story for you, Melody, as this was one of the issues you had to deal with while being here, and you've done such a good job. I hope you like it. It's called, 'The Glowing Orbs.'"

I'm beaming with pride, and I'm blushing, too.

• • • •

Far, far away in the land that bobbed in and out of view depending upon the sea mist, deep in the woods shone a radiant light. The light came from a glowing orb that surrounded each person who lived in the village beneath the tall trees. The glowing orbs shone more and more brightly as each person's self-esteem grew.

Every baby that was born into the village was different from the next—some had big heads and little noses, some had little heads and one ear, others had two noses and one eye, others had three eyes, one nostril and a tiny mouth, and still others had three ears, two noses and one eye. No one ever took any notice of the babies' features, for it was the glowing orb of light surrounding each infant that was considered beautiful, which made them all the same.

Miss Tina looks up at us and grins.

There were two tribes living side by side in the village, both from the same descendants, but they were as different as day and night. The elders of one tribe, the Luminums, shone brightly; their own orbs glowed around them and their children's orbs shone brightly as they praised them and taught them everything their own parents had shown them. But the elders of the other tribe, the Cimmerians, had no glowing light surrounding them, for some unspeak-

able wrong had been done to them hundreds of years ago. Although all babies were born with a glowing orb of light around them, little by little their light had dimmed until their form was in darkness, and all they could see was their features, the way they looked. They had lost the art of seeing true beauty, for the glowing orb of light was the beauty that the gods had intended all humans to see, not each other's features or physical form.

As the Luminum children grew, their light grew stronger with every new thing they achieved. Each time their parents said, "Good job," and spent time showing them how to do something new, they became more and more confident, and their light glowed more brightly. Laughter flowed from them as they sought to explore their world and capabilities without fear that they would fail, or that others would laugh at their efforts. There was never a day when doubt rested upon their shoulders, robbing them of the drive to learn more and more, and their glowing orb of light sparkled, letting them and everyone else know just how beautiful they were.

Although the Cimmerian children came into the world with the same glowing orb of light around them as the Luminums, their light gradually faded as their parents laughed when they fell over, jeered at their efforts to try new things and scornfully doused their desire to learn about the world around them. The children felt so bad that it was as if they didn't exist; they had no self-worth or self-esteem, and as their parents belittled them (as their own parents had done years before to them), they stopped trying to learn and shine. They focused only upon how they were seen by those around them.

Those Cimmerians who shared the same features as most of the other children banded together and believed that they were beautiful, and all those who weren't the same were considered ugly, without beauty of any kind. While they persecuted those who were different, they banded together feeling afraid that they too would be persecuted for their own subtle differences, and so they bullied and picked on all those who they thought didn't fit in with their idea of beauty.

The Luminum children, however, never noticed their physical features, for they were blessed with parents who fostered their self-esteem so that they believed in themselves and had the faith to be creative and try new experiences. Though they fell over many times and were filled with uncertainty when they learned something new, their parents picked them up and urged them forward, encouraging their efforts. With every new belief in themselves and every hurdle mastered, the orb surrounding them shone brighter, and their beauty sparkled, hiding their differing physical features.

The village became divided, with the Luminums and the Cimmerians having no way to speak to each other, each seeing the other as peculiar, their notion of beauty far removed from each other. The Luminum children made music, danced, painted and created art forms, while the Cimmerians stood in front of their mirrors attempting to look the same as the next, squashing any differences for fear of being persecuted and cast out of the village. Most of the Cimmerian children were miserable, for they feared the bullying they unleashed upon their own kind, and since no one paid them any attention, the orb of light that had been there at birth remained dimmed from view.

The village was destined to be divided for all time until a musician wandered down the path and walked into their midst. He was from a far off land that had no knowledge of the village or its inhabitants. As he walked, he sang and strummed his lute, and although he didn't know it, a glowing orb of light surrounded his body.

He didn't know what was considered beautiful, or that the Cimmerians and the Luminums saw beauty in entirely different ways, for he was eager to know all types of people no matter who they were.

The Luminums came out of their houses as they heard him singing and playing and saw the glow around his form, and the Cimmerians, curious about the newcomer, came out, too. He raised his hat to all those before him.

"Greetings," he said, "I have traveled far and I have gifts to share," dropping a large bag to the ground.

"What?" shouted the Cimmerian adults, hoping for fine clothes and jewels.

He sat among them and pulled off his boots to stretch his weary feet, and pulling a pipe from his bag he began to play. The Luminum children's lights glowed with pleasure while the Cimmerian children frowned with disappointment and scorn.

He stopped, suddenly confused, then stood up and reached into his bag. He walked around the children, who sat in a circle at his feet, and he gave each of them a musical instrument.

"Okay," he said, "let's make something beautiful."

The children looked at each other, still seeing the differences between themselves, but as the traveler began to play, he urged all the children to shake, rattle and tap their instruments. There was a great surge of rhythm, and laughter filled the air.

"Wonderful," he said to every child, and as his praise rested on the Cimmerian children, something amazing happened. A faint glow began to shimmer around them. The Luminum children smiled at them, recognizing the beauty they knew and were used to.

The Cimmerian parents shook their heads in confusion...what was happening?

"Let's do another song," the traveler cried. "Sing and play with all your heart."

The children did just that, and even though some made mistakes and missed a beat, or sang out of tune, hit their drums at the wrong time and sang with thorns in their throats, the traveler smiled at them and encouraged the children to grow, enjoy, and learn.

"Yes, yes," he shouted. "Truly wonderful," and as he praised the children's efforts to learn a new song, the light around the Luminum children's bodies shone brightly, and sitting next to them, the Cimmerian children began to glow, too.

Their parents were perplexed and fearful. What was happening to their children? They were starting to glow with self-esteem and their physical features were diminishing. Suddenly all the children of the village began to look the same, all radiating an exquisite glow, the beauty of self-expression and confidence.

One by one the Cimmerian parents began to cry, for how they had longed for someone like the traveler to help them to glow with the light and "shine" that they had seen in their newborn babies and in the Luminum tribe.

Every villager sang and danced throughout the night, and as the Cimmerians' orbs shone brighter and brighter, they shed their self-doubt and false belief that it was looks that made one beautiful; and so the traveler slipped silently away, his work complete.

The next morning all the children of the village shone in the sunlight, the glowing orb around their bodies shining and vibrant. The Cimmerian children shone as much as the Luminum children and they became close friends, not being the slightest bit concerned with physical features anymore.

The elders of the village held a meeting, for now that everyone acknowledged their "shine," their glowing orb of light shone brightly and their physical features faded from view. The gods had meant it to be this way, so as those who had only known the darkness came to see their own light and worth, the two tribes were no longer divided. They agreed that beauty was to be defined as the glowing orb of light that every human child was born with.

So after long deliberations they became united, and from that day forth all the villagers were known as Luminerians. They no longer focused on physical features as a source of beauty and acceptance, but saw the glow as being beautiful, the glow that every human being has, who lets his light shine. They recognized what the gods had intended, that it is the "shine" inside a person that makes them truly beautiful.

• • • •

Miss Tina smiles and put the pages down.

"Do you like it?" she asks me.

"I love it. May I take it home with me?"

"Yes, I wrote it for you. Do you understand it, Melody? It doesn't matter what physical features you have; what's attractive to others is whether you shine, whether your lights are on, and on Show Night you showed everyone here that your lights *are* on, shining brightly, and you are truly beautiful."

I'm crying, I can't help it, and she comes over to me and holds me.

"I'm going to miss you all so badly," I sob.

"We're all still here for you, you know that."

• • • •

The time flies by and too soon Mom and Danny are here to pick me up. Freddie hugs me and says she'll call, and Rick hugs me too, and says he'll come and see me tomorrow so that I can meet the other two members of our band. He still doesn't kiss me, and I figure it's because my mom's here. Miss Tina walks us out to Mom's car, and I wave out of the back window until I can't see her anymore.

Danny turns around in his seat, and says, "Mel, you'll love it where we're living, it's really cool."

He sounds happy and some of my fears slip away. If *he* likes it then it'll be all right by me. I can't think of anything to say, as I'm full of feelings that jostle to be felt first. I want to cry but I feel excited too, I feel sad but I also feel happy, but most of all I can't wait for Rick to come over tomorrow.

Mom pulls up in front of a big house.

"Is this it?" I ask, dumbfounded. It's very different from our broken-down little house.

"It's cool," Danny says, opening my door.

"Wow."

Mom opens the front door and Donnie comes out to meet us.

"Hi," he says, "I'm Donnie. Good to have you here. This is your home now, so…" he shrugs, suddenly stuck for words, "…make yourself at home."

He puts his hand out to shake mine and I like him immediately.

"I've got a surprise for you," Mom says. "I hope you like it."

She disappears, and as she comes back through the door, a squeal seeps out of me. In her arms is a tiny, black Labrador puppy.

"He's yours, baby. I'm so sorry about what happened to Buster."

"It's not your fault, Mom, I don't blame you at all."

She hands him to me and he licks my face all over, and I giggle.

"Thanks, Mom, he's gorgeous."

Danny says, "Come and see your room," and I follow him up the stairs.

"Isn't this amazing? I wish Mom had left Dad ages ago," he says.

It's fabulous—wide stairs, clean, gentle colored walls, plants growing everywhere, and no dust. He takes me to a door down a wide hall that has a name plaque hanging on it, saying "Melody's room." He opens the door.

"Yours!" he says, smiling at me.

I can't believe it. My room is beautiful and it has a bathroom. I don't have to share anymore. In the corner is a doggy bed. "Here Ricky," I name my dog, "this is your bed. Look."

Donnie brings my stuff upstairs and places my bags just inside the door.

"Danny brought most of your stuff. Do you like your room?"

"I love it, thanks, and thanks for the dog, it means so much to me."

"Oh, it's nothing. I just hope he helps to make up for...well, you know."

"Thank you for letting us come to live here. We'll be good, I promise."

He waves his hand in my direction. "Oh, hush. You have no idea how happy your mom is that you both want to come and live with us. I know this must have been a bit of a shock."

"I wish she'd done it earlier; then she wouldn't have been so unhappy."

I don't say, "Then we wouldn't have been so unhappy either," because there's no point, and it would've been rude anyway...and I don't want to be rude to this man. He seems really nice.

I go back downstairs and Mom's sitting in the most

amazing kitchen I've ever seen.

"Miss Tina talked to me while you were packing, and she said that you did a really good job in class this morning and wrote an excellent essay. I'm really proud of you, baby, and I think it's a great idea to have a cell phone on you at all times so that you can reach out if things get tough. Donnie's going to let you take his to school tomorrow, and he'll buy one for you and Danny tomorrow some time when he gets a break. Is that okay?"

I put Ricky down on the floor and hug her.

"I love you, Mom. I'm sorry I've been so moody sometimes, and mean. It's just been hard at school; the other kids hate me and it hurts."

I don't say that they hate me because I look like my mom and I'm ugly, because I've finally *heard* everything Miss Tina and my new friends have said to me; I'm not ugly. A strange thing is happening as I look into my mom's eyes. She doesn't look ugly anymore; she looks radiant. I know what's different—her lights are on, she's happy, and I know exactly what Miss Tina's story is about.

I rush upstairs to find Miss Tina's story so that I can show it to Mom, and she doesn't seem to know what to say after she's read it. She just blows her nose.

The phone rings and Donnie says it's for me.

"Hello?"

"Hey, Melody, it's Larry. Rick called me and said that you're coming back to school. Great. I don't know how you feel about it, but do you want me to stop by in the morning and walk with you to school?"

I've been so scared about going back to school. I can't be sure that I won't run away when faced with all those taunts and nasty comments. I shudder; I wonder if anyone knows that I tried to kill myself. I hope not because I can only imagine the nasty things they'll say.

"Oh, yes please. Do you know where I live?"

"No."

Nor do I.

"Mom," I call, feeling a little silly. "Where do I live?"

I give him directions and hang up, feeling so relieved.

"Mom, d'you know that I'm going to be in a band?" Donnie looks up from his paper. "Well, that was Larry who's in one of my classes at school. He plays lead guitar...he's amazing. I've never heard anyone play like him. He's going to stop by in the morning and walk with me to school."

"That's nice."

"Mom, I'm really scared about going back to school."

I don't want to tell her, but Miss Tina says that I should express my feelings.

"The kids pick on me badly. Can I please wear makeup? My friend Freddie showed me how to put it on so that it '*enhances*' the way you look and doesn't make you look 'painted' or cheap." I feel a sudden pang of longing for my friend and her playfulness.

I swear that Miss Tina has spoken to Mom because all she says is "Yes, dear. Do you know what colors suit you?"

I tell her everything Freddie said her sister had taught her. "She's going to be a makeup artist one day."

"Donnie's barbecuing tonight, so how about we go and pick up the makeup you need while he and Danny make dinner? There's a drugstore just down the road."

She laughs as Donnie raises an eyebrow and winks at her. I've never seen my mom look so happy, and something that lives very deep inside me swells until I'm choked and can barely speak.

"Mom, I'm so happy for you. He's great. The house is great. I wish you'd followed your heart earlier. You deserve the best."

"Stop it," she says playfully, slapping my hand. "You'll have me weeping."

"That's fine. Miss Tina says you should show your feelings."

We spend an hour in the drugstore where a lady with too much makeup on tries to tell us how to look just like her. I find the shades that Freddie told me suit my eyes and a lipstick to die for, and Mom says, "You'll want a makeup bag to put it in. Choose one you like."

It feels like Christmas and it seems like Mom's trying too hard to make things okay.

"Mom, you don't have to do this; I'm just happy that you want us to come and live with you and Donnie..."

She silences me as we pull into the drive.

"Listen, Melly, I've made mistakes. I tried to protect you from the pain I endured, and yet you've suffered other pains. I've always said that you couldn't wear makeup without really thinking about it...my parents said the same to me, but there's no real reason why you can't wear it if it makes you feel good about yourself. Perhaps you can show me how to put it on so that I don't feel as if I belong to a circus."

She smiles at me as she takes the key out of the ignition, and I smile back, for something wonderful is happening between my mom and me.

I wake up after a restless night. I miss Rick and Freddie, Tammy, Julie and Paul, and Miss Tina. I'm scared stiff. I know Larry's going to take me to school and I'm grateful, but the bullies think he's a nerd, too. I try and chase away the image of us hanging on to each other, two nerds huddled together, against a barrage of bullying.

I shower in my own bathroom and dress, spending ages doing my makeup, wiping it off twice and starting again before I'm satisfied with it; well, as satisfied as I can be. I take one final look in the mirror, but I'm still not really happy. At Beach Haven I knew that, whatever I looked like, I was "okay" with the other kids, but I'm going to school, a place where the rules aren't the same.

"Melly," Mom calls up the stairs, "I have to go now. I'll see you later. Have a good day and call me if you need to. My number's on the table."

"Okay, have a good one."

I go back into the bathroom and try to do something with the piece of hair that flops over my face, but it's a wasted effort; it was okay the way it was.

The doorbell rings.

Danny opens the door.

"Hi."

"Hi."

It must be Larry. I grab my school bag and go downstairs.

I can't see anyone in the hall. Ricky bounds over to me and jumps up, longing to lick my face but I don't let him, given that I've just spent two hours trying to fix it.

"Get down, you silly little dog, *down*." I shoo him away as I go into the kitchen and there—sitting at the table—is Rick.

"They let me go last night instead of today so I thought I would come and take you to school."

Larry's sitting there next to Donnie, who's taken a couple of hours off work to help me. They're grinning at me, but what makes tears come into my eyes is that my brother—my brother, who has never wanted to be associated with me at school—is sitting there waiting to help me go back to face the bullies.

Chapter Nine

A thrill courses through me and I cry out loud.

Donnie says, "Those kids had better look out; you've got four men to escort you to school."

And Danny says, " And two who'll be with you until home time."

I want to cry but I don't dare, as I want my make-up to stay intact.

Donnie piles us all into his BMW and my stomach's going crazy with fear, but it gets worse as we drive and he parks right outside the school steps.

"C'mon," he says, "we're taking you to the school office to sign you back in."

As I walk up the steps, kids stare at me and whisper. Some laugh, some look away, but they move back as Donnie leads the way.

I try to hold my head up high and think about all the "affirmation leaves" on my Self-Esteem Tree. I am not cold, barren and bare. I'm scared, but I'm not that winter tree standing naked and alone.

As kids start to snicker and say in a loud voice, "That's the girl who tried to hang herself because her father sexually abused her," Rick says, "Don't listen, Mel, don't listen. They don't even have their facts right. None of them is worth reacting to, so ignore it. We're here, we're with you."

He's just given me an "affirmation leaf" after a couple of mine have been pulled off by the kids jeering at me.

We walk through the school doors and go straight to the office, where Donnie takes charge.

He says, "This is my stepdaughter. She's been out of school for a few weeks and I'm ready to sign her back in, and I want her twin brother to be in her class, okay? I trust there'll be no problem with that."

He sounds very strong, and I love how he's just called me his stepdaughter.

There are kids standing in groups outside the school office, staring and whispering...some are laughing.

The staff get the principal and he comes out of his office looking perplexed, but after Donnie tells him that Danny and I *have* to be in the same class, he says, "Very well, whatever we can do to help, sir."

Donnie signs the papers and I'm told to go to my class. Danny comes with me but I'm still terrified.

Larry's already gone to class, and knowing that he's there is the only thing that keeps me from snapping and losing control of myself.

There are still kids in groups hanging around the hall laughing at me. I'm panic struck and I know that Donnie and Rick can see it.

"Can I have a hug?" Donnie asks, and I allow myself to lean against him for his strength and comfort.

Danny's waiting. "We have to go, Mel, or we'll get detention."

"Go now, Mel," Rick says. "I'm going to meet you here after school and then we're going to start practicing, and you'll get to meet the other members of the band. So no crying or you'll wreck your beautiful voice." He wags his finger at me playfully.

I love him so much, and when he gives me a hug, I melt into his arms and long to be there forever. I can hear the kids gasp when they see me in Rick's arms.

Rick and Donnie say goodbye and promise to meet me after school, and then suddenly it's just Danny and me.

"Are you ready?" he says.

I nod, although it's a lie; I don't think I'll ever be ready to face this.

I follow him down the stairs towards our classroom, but as we get to the door, I freak.

"I can't go in there."

Danny holds my hand and refuses to let go. "You can do this. Just stay by me."

He knocks, and then pushes the door open with his feet as his hands are holding me tightly.

"Sorry we're late," he says.

"Never mind. I'm glad you could both join us. I believe Larry has reserved two seats for you. Sit down and let's start."

There are whispers, soft ones, which I can handle by letting them go over my head, but the louder ones are harder to ignore.

"Hey, Danny, what you doing? Come back here with us, there's a spare seat here," says a skinny girl with long blonde hair, who's wearing a lot of eye makeup.

"No, I want to sit with my sister, but thanks."

The room falls silent and I'm more thankful to Danny than I can ever say. He stood up for me even though his own popularity is in jeopardy by siding with nerdy old me.

We sit down in the front row, and I sit between Larry and Danny, grateful for their presence.

The teacher talks but I don't hear a word he's saying. My head is spinning and my ears feel as if they've grown twice their normal size, for sounds that I would not normally hear seem magnified to me. I can hear kids whispering behind me, and although I can't hear what they're saying, I just know they're talking about me.

"Turn to page 397," the teacher says, and Larry has to nudge me to bring my spinning head and sensitive ears back to the front row. He smiles at me and scribbles on his book, "Are you okay? My fists are ready if you're not."

I giggle and suddenly my ears feel the right size again and I can't hear the whispering behind me any more.

At break I need to go to the bathroom; Danny and Larry walk with me. Danny's telling him about Mom moving in with Donnie and how fantastic his house is, but even though I'm listening, the only thing I can really hear is the group of girls behind us laughing.

"Look at her hair—what a mess."

"I'm surprised she's got the nerve to come back to school."

"She wouldn't if she knew what everyone thinks about her."

My stomach lurches and I rush into the bathroom and throw up. I know that Danny and Larry are trying to help me, but even though they're standing right next to me, it doesn't stop the kids from picking on me. It hurts so badly and I can't help the tears from falling while I'm locked in the cubicle.

I hear the girls come into the bathroom and I know that they know I'm in here...they saw me come in.

"What a slut. I heard that she offered the boys sex for money, that's what Jeff said. She's a whore, an ugly whore. Who'd want to go with her?"

"I'd die if I were her, I'd just die."

"Well, they say she tried to kill herself."

"Shame she didn't try harder."

They all laugh and I clamp my hand over my mouth to stifle the sobs that are desperate to leave my body and fill the chilly bathroom.

"C'mon, let's go," one of them says and they leave, laughing as they go.

I slump to the floor and sob my heart out, longing for Freddie and Rick, and Miss Tina. I miss Beach Haven so much. It's the only place where I've ever felt as if I mean something to myself and to others. I feel like a piece of dirt sitting on the toilet floor, too scared to open the door and show myself.

I'm in here for ages and the bell rings, but I can't come out.

The bathroom door opens. "Mel, are you still in here?" Danny says.

I'm so relieved it's him that I open the door and fall into him.

"What the..."

"I'm going home," I sob, unable to get any breath.

"What happened? What did they do?"

"I'm going home."

I push past him through the door and run from the building with Danny and Larry running after me.

"Wait," they shout. "Mel, stop."

I can't, I have to get as far away as possible from this hateful place with its hateful kids.

They catch up with me and Danny grabs me.

"STOP!"

I'm crying so badly that he shakes me and looks really scared.

"I'm taking her home, Larry. You go back to school and tell the principal what's happened."

"Okay," he says, looking worried.

Danny puts his arm around me and takes me home to Donnie's house, and as I stumble up the stairs I can hear him on the phone to Mom.

Ricky leaps upon to my bed and seems to sense how desperately miserable I am and nestles his wet nose into my face, licking my salty tears away.

Mom comes home, so does Donnie, and it all pours out of me, what those horrible girls said while I was trapped in the bathroom cubicle. Mom holds me as I cry, and I know that my "beautiful voice" will be a ragged washboard with all the crying I've done, but not even the thought of Rick makes me feel any better.

Mom stays with me all day, and I'm grateful. Donnie owns the company and tells her to take the day off. She tells me how the kids used to bully her, too, when she was a kid, and she tells me that she knows just what I'm feeling.

I'm still crying when the principal calls the house and I can hear Mom talking to him.

"Yes...yes...well, no, not really...well, yes, that may work...okay, thank you."

I blow my nose and wipe my eyes.

"That was your principal. He says that he understands what you're going through, but he thinks that the only way to beat the bullies is to stand up to them and not give in."

"I can't go back, Mom, I just can't."

"Baby, I know it's hard, but I agree with him. It's what I had to do. It was hard, really hard, but they stopped when they saw that it didn't bother me."

I'm crying hard again. She doesn't understand, she can't, or she wouldn't make me go back there again. She takes my hands and looks into my eyes.

"Baby, you have to learn how to act. You may be dying inside but you need to let them think that nothing they say means anything at all to you. It's the only way. Bullies thrive on seeing their victims suffer, and as soon as they see that they can't hurt you anymore, they'll give up, I promise you. It's how it was for me and it's how it's been since time began. I hate it, but it's part of human nature."

She holds me and I know from her voice that no amount of pleading will change her mind.

"I went on a vacation once in Spain and was up in the mountains. We visited a farm where they made goat's cheese and wine, and while my mom went on a tour of the farm, I watched the animals in their pen. There were chickens in the goat's pen amongst the beautiful newborn baby goats. Some stood up immediately and the chickens walked away from them, but those that didn't stand up were pecked at. The chickens pecked and pecked until the poor creatures couldn't stand up; they were pecking them to death. I couldn't stand it so I ran to find the farmer to tell him what was happening, but he did nothing. All he said was, "It needs to stand up for itself or it won't make it." That was all he said, but his words stuck with me. You have to stand up for yourself, Melly; even though it's hard and you're afraid, you just have to. We're all here for you but it's only you that can make those bullies—those chickens—back off."

I know she's right, and I hate it. I feel a terrible sense of hopelessness come over me. How am I going to do it? It hurts too much.

"The principal says that Miss Tina is coming to the school tomorrow to hold her group, and he says to call her and ask if she can help at all."

I feel a flicker of hope.

Mom's on the phone and eventually she hands it over to me. It's my beloved Miss Tina. I start crying all over again.

"Sweetheart, listen," she says, her voice so soft and warm, "I'm coming to school tomorrow. I'll see you there, okay? You can do this, Melody, you can. Just think of all the 'affirmation leaves' you have on your Self-Esteem Tree; don't let a few spiteful, insecure girls and boys make your leaves fall off."

I laugh at the pictures she makes come into my

head. I'm so glad that she's there for me on the end of a phone.

I know it's only midday but I sleep for hours, exhausted from crying, until Mom, who didn't go back to work because she wanted to make sure that I was okay, opens my bedroom door.

Rick and Larry come in and sit on my bed.

"Babe!" Rick says, his eyebrows knotting with concern. "Danny and Larry told me. Tough, eh?"

I sit up, suddenly scared that he'll see the real me, without my hair done, smudged makeup and eyes that look like burnt out firecrackers in the snow.

"School can be tough, but you're tougher. C'mon. Get up. I said that I was going to pick you up for band practice and that's what I'm going to do. Okay, it wasn't from school, but hey, I can compromise. You've got five minutes. We'll wait for you downstairs, okay?"

I get up right away and wash my face, trying to ignore my horrible red piggy eyes. I don't have time to redo my makeup as he's shouting up the stairs, "C'mon, we're leaving now."

I run out of the house. Mom's smiling, so's Danny. I feel my heart soar. Hang the bullies; I bet none of them feels the way I'm feeling right now.

Rick can drive, so we get into his car and Larry lets me sit in the front as if I'm Rick's girlfriend. It feels wonderful sitting next to him, and I don't care about the bullies right this minute. I'm in heaven.

He pulls off the road into the drive of a huge house and I know my mouth gapes open in awe.

"You live here?" I ask stupidly.

"Yep."

He pulls up in front of a building. "This is my shed."

"It's a *shed*?" I say flabbergasted. "It's a house."

He laughs and parks the car. I can already hear music coming from the inside of his "shed," and I follow him through the door.

It's set out like a stage, and as soon as the two boys see him they stop playing.

"Hey, Pete, Al, this is Mel. She's amazing, you should hear her sing."

I'm scared; my voice has been desecrated through crying all day and I doubt if I have any vocal chords left. They raise their hands, say "Hi," and go back to playing without giving me a second glance, and I'm relieved.

Rick stands me in front of them and puts a microphone in my hand.

"Okay, Mel, we've got a gig coming up in a couple of weeks so we need to practice hard, all right."

They play and I sing until the sun goes down, and all thoughts of the bullies have evaporated from my mind. They don't exist; the only thing that exists for me is Rick and what we're creating here in this "shed" beneath the moonlight.

• • • •

Larry calls for me in the morning and Donnie takes us to school again; I feel nervous, but knowing that Miss Tina is going to be in school today helps. As we walk past the school office she sees us and comes out to say "Hi." I'm so pleased to see her, and she asks me how my Self-Esteem Tree is as she hugs me. Kids walk by, whispering and staring.

"Well, it was cold, barren and bare yesterday morning, but now it's got lots of leaves on it."

Danny's face screws up into the shape of a question mark.

"Good. Your mom told me that you were practicing with the band last night. How did it go?"

"It was unbelievable." I'm so excited about it that I don't really listen to Miss Tina talking about how to deal with bullies. I'm surprised that I'm not a quivering wreck, considering what happened at school yesterday, but my whole being is so saturated with Rick and the band that I feel as if nothing the bullies say can touch me. I'm surprised by my feelings since I was devastated yesterday; I guess I had a whole lot more "affirmation leaves" stuck onto my Self-Esteem Tree after last night's practice with the band.

Danny and I go to class, and he positions me between himself and Larry.

"Are you okay? Wasn't last night fantastic? You have the most unbelievable voice I've ever heard," Larry says.

He says it as the teacher enters the room and everyone has gotten quiet except him; what he says echoes around the room.

I smile at him and open my book. Somehow I don't hear any whisperings behind me. Danny and Larry keep looking at me with worry on their faces, which tells me that there *are* whisperings floating to the front row where the nerds sit, but I don't hear them. I'm in Rick's "shed" with Larry, Pete and Al, creating something that's beyond words, something that the kids behind me can't penetrate with their snide, nasty remarks.

At break the kids walk behind us laughing, but this time I'm not going to the bathroom for any-thing, even if I have to hold it or wet myself. In front of them I call Freddie, and we laugh and joke about her falling flat on her ass while jiving with Tammy.

She tells me she loves me and I tell her I love her, too. The kids listening to me don't know who I'm talking to, but they know by my face that someone, somewhere, cares about me enough for me to say publicly, "I love you, too." They don't know that it's not a boyfriend. They shut up, and one or two of them look at me hard. I wish Freddie could see me and hear what's going on; she'd laugh.

Miss Tina said that if I don't react to the bullies' taunts, they will get bored and stop, and I think she might be right because, as I laugh with Freddie, with

Danny and Larry by my side, they shrug and walk away, saying, "Whatever!"

• • • •

It's been two weeks since I came back to school and it's been hard—real hard—but every day, as I get more and more focused on practicing for our first gig, the bullies mean nothing to me. They watch Larry and me pouring over music scores and one or two say nasty things like, "Hook nose has got a boyfriend," or "They deserve each other; two nerds together." Larry grabs my arm if I start to react, and he tells me they're not worth it, and he's right.

We practice and practice every night. It's wonderful, exhilarating, yet exhausting, but I love it and it becomes my life. If I ever had any doubts about where my future lies, I don't now; it's in music—music, and the bond it creates with other people, is the only future for me.

Donnie comes to our practices sometimes and writes songs for us to try out at our gig. He's smart and can play almost every instrument. I think he's awesome, and while I'm thinking that he's awesome, I don't think about my dad at all, and that feels safe and right.

Today is the last day of school and it's my birthday. I'll be fifteen, I'm so relieved that this year is over. I pray that some of the kids will move and change schools so that in the fall there'll be new kids, and things will have changed.

Tonight is our first gig so my mind's fixed on rehearsing, and I don't care about the last day of school and all the celebrations. The girls in the back row go on and on about what they're going to wear to the end-of-school-year party. I ignore them as their sarcasm bites into me when they ask if I'm coming and bringing my nerdy boyfriend...they mean Larry. Larry hisses at me, "Ignore them," but this time I can't.

"No, actually, I've got somewhere loads better to go."

They walk off laughing at me, and I want to do something rude with my finger, but I don't because Larry's watching.

We're allowed out of school early today. I'm very pleased because it means we can practice longer. Larry walks home with me and I drop my bag off, then we walk to Rick's house. His car is parked outside the "shed" and I almost run to the door...I can't wait to see him.

I don't knock but just push the door open, and suddenly my whole world freezes and splinters into a million icy shards that pierce my heart. He's on the couch, kissing a girl.

I know my face betrays me and I utter a strangled scream before running out of the door. I can hear him calling after me, but I run, sobbing.

I don't remember getting home, but I stagger upstairs to my room and cry like I've never cried in my whole life; I cry even harder than when Buster was killed, and harder than when I was shamed by Jeff and his friend. This is the worst I've ever felt, and the pain is so bad that I want to die, despite everything Miss Tina's told me...her words are just out of reach, hidden by the agony in my heart.

Danny opens my bedroom door and sits on my bed looking wretched, not knowing what to do.

"Mel, what's the matter? What's happened?"

I can't answer him and I'm only vaguely aware that there's fear in his voice. He goes downstairs to call Mom on the phone. He comes back upstairs and sits on my bed with his hand awkwardly resting upon my back in an attempt to comfort me.

I can't stop crying. Every leaf on my Self-Esteem Tree has fallen off and I'm the same ugly nerd with sunken piggy eyes, hooked nose and crooked teeth that I was when I first went to Beach Haven. Everything's been a lie. Rick's a lie. He's everything to me; it's he who has told me I'm beautiful, who's put leaves on my tree so that I can feel good about myself. But all the time I thought I was his girlfriend, he's been cheating on me and has got someone else.

I feel so humiliated and stupid, as destroyed as I felt after Jeff and his friend had used me and everyone else knew about it. The band must know about Rick's girlfriend but none of them told me about it...they must be laughing at me. My dreams of singing are squashed, flattened forever. I'll never sing again; my heart's broken. I'll never love anyone again, ever.

These thoughts drown me, and by the time Mom comes home, I'm hysterical and hurt so bad that I'm screaming.

"Stop," Mom says, shaking me. "Stop it, stop it," and she slaps my face.

I shudder with shock, and we stare at each other, horrified, for an endless second before I tremble and cry again.

She holds me and croons into my ear, "Oh, baby, you'll be all right, it's okay."

Doesn't she know that my entire world has crumbled? I've never known such desolation. I can't go on, I just can't. I don't know what to do and I'm scared that if she leaves me alone I'll end my life, that's how bad I feel. And yet I know I can't do that because it would hurt Mom and Danny too much. So I feel trapped, trapped in a place where misery and pain fill my soul, and living feels like a waiting game until I can be released from its agonies.

My tears roll down my face and blur my vision. There's a figure in the doorway, and suddenly Mom pulls away from me, saying, "Sort it out, both of you, okay?"

Rick closes the door behind him and comes over to my bed. He sits. He looks as bad as I do.

"How could you?" I blurt out angrily.

"Mel, I haven't done anything wrong."

"What d'you mean you haven't done anything wrong? You were kissing another girl."

"She's my girlfriend, Mel. We've been together for three years. I love her."

"But I thought...I thought *I* was your girlfriend. You told me I was beautiful; you lied to me."

"You *are* beautiful, inside and out, but Melly, I've never lied to you, never."

"You told me Jenny had gone."

He reaches out for my hand and there's pain on his face, terrible pain, almost as bad as mine. His eyes brim with tears.

"Jenny's my sister. She drowned, and it was my fault."

"Your sister?"

"Yes, my sister. She was fourteen and ..." he clears his throat in an effort not to cry, "and she looks just like you. Everything about you reminds me of Jenny. Sometimes it's so painful to look at you, not only because you are so beautiful in your own right but because you also remind me so much of her."

He wipes his eyes with the back of his hands.

"Melly, I've never lied to you, I haven't. I shouldn't have dumped my stuff on you when we sat on the beach and you hugged me. I'm sorry, I didn't mean to lose control, but sometimes it's just so hard, especially when you are so like her. Please forgive me."

My head's spinning. We had hugged on the beach, and I thought it was because he wanted me to be his girlfriend, but then a nagging doubt reminds me that even after that beautiful moment, he didn't hold my hand or try to kiss me, as I hoped he would.

"I love you, Mel, believe me, I love you. You are the most beautiful person inside and out that I've ever met, and I wish with all my heart that Jenny was still alive so that she could meet you. I've never lied to you, babe, I haven't...I wouldn't."

My mind is racing. He's telling me that he loves me, and I believe him because I can see it on his face. But it's not the kind of love that boyfriends and girlfriends share, and up until now I didn't know there were different types of love.

Images of us at Beach Haven flash before me, and although he told me how wonderful he thought I was, he never actually made any attempt to hold me, kiss me or touch me.

A wave of humiliation sweeps over me as I feel stupid for thinking that he could possibly want me to be his girlfriend. I don't know what to say. I never asked him why he was at Beach Haven, I just assumed that it was because his girlfriend had left him, and he was so nice to me that I thought he wanted me. It never occurred to me that he had a girlfriend and was being nice to me because I am who I am.

As I think these thoughts, something dawns on me. Freddie and I talked a lot about how boys will be nice to you if they think you'll let them kiss you or touch you; she said "they only want one thing." But Rick is sitting on my bed telling me that he loves me, despite having a girlfriend, and that he has no intention of only wanting "one thing."

I don't know what's happening to me, and I think I'm probably too young to understand it all—nor do I want to at the moment for it all seems too hard—but something seeps through my pain and rests next to my heart. Rick loves me for me, not for my body or sex...he loves me for me.

My humiliation leaves me and I sit on the edge of the bed sniffing, my hooked nose running, and my sunken piggy eyes red-raw. I dare to look at him, and I see a desperate pleading in his eyes that says, "Please believe me, it's true."

I can't think of a thing to say so I'm quiet and so is he. There's a noise outside my door, and I imagine my mom's listening through the gap.

He finally speaks. "Melly, we have something fantastic going on, utterly wonderful. You are so beautiful, you fit perfectly in our band...it's your band, too. There's nothing and no one that can stop me loving you, so let's go and practice. Please, babe, it's only six hours away."

I don't know what's happened inside me, because half an hour ago I was ready to kill myself again. Yet now I feel as if something "grown up" has happened to me, and even though it still hurts really badly, all my "affirmation leaves" are still on my Self-Esteem Tree.

I nod. "Okay. I'm sorry; I shouldn't have assumed. It was silly of me. I should have asked you why you were at Beach Haven."

"No, I'm sorry, babe, I should have been more clear...I guess I was always so reluctant to talk about Jenny's death, or anything else. I should have told the group about Becky (I know I wince at her name), and Jenny's death, but I just found it all so difficult." He's quiet for a moment, then he says gently, "Melly, you've helped me so much; I can't begin to tell you. Thank you, baby."

We turn to each other and hug as if our lives depend upon it, which they probably do at this moment.

Chapter Ten

Four hours later Freddie bangs on our door.

"I'm here to help Mel get ready for the gig," I hear her tell my mom.

I hang over the stairs, "Freddie! I'm so glad you're here."

Mom and Donnie go into the living room to leave us alone. Danny's spending the night with his friend. I think he's going to the stupid end-of-school-year party but didn't want to tell me in case I was upset or felt left out. I don't care, I really don't.

Freddie drops her bag on my bed. "Right, I've brought all my wardrobe for you to choose from."

She dumps it out and there's everything on my bed, stuff I've never been allowed to wear before, stuff I've only dreamed about. I allow her to dress me and do my makeup, and then she does something wild with my hair.

"What d'you think?" she asks, standing behind me in the bathroom as we look into the mirror.

I can't believe it; I look like someone else, yet I can still see me, the ugly nerd...but I'm not ugly at all. I can't deny it anymore; yes, my features are unique, different, but as I look at myself I have to admit that Freddie has made me look stunning.

"I can't believe it," I say. "You're so smart. You've made me look...well, um...great."

She gives me a little shake. "Mel, I've done nothing. You're beautiful because you're beautiful, that's all."

Donnie shouts up the staircase, "Are you girls ready?"

"Your stepdad's taking us to the gig, and I told you, you can't get rid of me—I'm going to be in the wings. I'm here for you, Mel; anything you want, you just let me know."

I didn't know that Donnie was going to take us to the gig. I guess I've been crying so much today that I haven't heard anything properly.

Mom's dressed up, and so is Donnie. They look great.

"Are you going out to dinner?" I ask.

"Well, we're kind of hungry," she says. "C'mon, you're going to be late."

I sit in the back of the car with Freddie, and as we giggle I feel overwhelmed with love for her. I can't believe that in one day I can feel so many different emotions, all as strong as each other. I look at Mom in the front of the car and wonder if she feels as alive as I feel right now, and as I think about it I see her glance at Donnie with a look that excludes me, and I know she does.

Freddie grabs my hand and holds it tight as we turn the corner.

Donnie pulls up in front of my school steps.

I'm instantly confused; then as the realization dawns on me, I'm horrified—no, terrified.

"What? Why have you brought me here?" I say stupidly. "No, no. No way."

Freddie still holds my hand and refuses to let go.

"Baby, this is your gig. The end-of-school-year party needs a band and you're it."

"No! No, I can't. I can't."

"Yes, you can, and you will. Miss Tina's coming, Julie, Tammy and Paul, they're all coming, even though they don't go to school here, and your Mom and Dad are staying."

"You're not going out to dinner?" I ask, feeling conned.

"Not dressed like this," Mom says.

I feel cornered, yet they're all smiling at me, urging me on.

"Mel, you can do this standing on your head; just think you're in the shower. It's your chance to show everyone in this school that you are beautiful inside and out. You have enough people giving you 'affirmation leaves' so that you won't ever feel cold, barren and bare."

Mom and Donnie look at us quizzically.

"Don't ask," Freddie says, grinning, "I'll explain later."

They don't even wait for me to reply before they get out of the car, and Rick's dad pulls up beside us.

I don't know what to think. My head's spinning and I'm more afraid than I can possibly say. All those girls who have spent weeks deciding what to wear to this party will be there, and all the boys who laugh at me and say such terrible things will be there waiting to witness my humiliation. I wish I'd never agreed to be in this band.

Rick comes over to me. "I'm sorry I didn't tell you, babe, but I figured you wouldn't be very happy. Listen, I know how it's been for you in this place, I *do* know. Kids used to bully me because I had long hair and was 'only interested in one thing...'" my heart lurches, "music, that's all...well, and my little sister, Jenny."

I don't know what to do or say; I can't walk off as I can't let my friends down, but my stomach is sick and there's bile in my throat.

Freddie says, "Babe, you look fantastic. Everything is fantastic, especially your voice, so get out there and show those bullies the real you. I'll be in the wings and you've got four gorgeous guys out there with you."

She digs me in the ribs, and says, "Girl, what's the matter with you? Any girl would give anything to be you. Now, just go."

Mom's nodding at me, so I let Rick and Freddie lead me up the steps into the school.

There's no one there yet and Al tells me they're not due for an hour and a half, so there's time to set up and practice.

I've never known ninety minutes to go by so fast and, although the curtains are closed on the stage, I can hear the kids filing into the school hall. My stomach is churning with terror. Freddie is by my side constantly, even when I want to go to the bathroom; it's like she's my bodyguard or something, or rather my soul-guard...that would be more like it.

I'm sick, really sick, and vomit.

"Girl, you're determined that I'm going to earn my place in your band, aren't you?" as she cleans up after me. I'm humiliated, but grateful. I cup my hands and drink loads of cold water; then Freddie fixes my lipstick.

I can hear music playing and Rick is peeping through the long dusty curtains.

"It's jam packed," he says.

"Hush," says Freddie, giving him a warning glance. "Go on, Melly, we love you, remember that. You've got the most fabulous voice, so go out there and let them have it."

She pushes me onto the stage and Rick holds my

hand, hugs me, tells me I'm truly beautiful, and stands me in front of a mic. I can hear someone saying, "And now, welcome 'A Month Of Sundays...'"

The curtains pull back and I can see Donnie introducing us with a "Go get 'em" look on his face as he turns to face us.

I'm frozen, frozen to the core. I can't move, for there in front of me are all the girls from the back row and the boys that chase after them. They look up and then turn to each other with shocked surprise. Some point at me.

My stomach's in shreds. I can't run because that would be worse than sticking this out, but I am absolutely terrified. Rick calls me, away from his mic. "Mel, focus on me, pretend you're in the shower, ignore everyone out there. Remember your Self-Esteem Tree." He plucks a string on his guitar and it howls around the school hall, silencing the shocked murmuring.

I turn to my side to do as he says, trying desperately to concentrate on everything we've practiced. Although my voice is croaky to start with, as I look at Rick I relax, and by the time we start the second number, I feel able to face the front.

The groups of girls in front of the stage all hope to make eye contact with the boys in the band, and out of the corner of my eye I see the girl that Rick was kissing. I try to manage a smile at her and, whether she sees it or not, she smiles at me. Next to her are

Mom and Donnie and Miss Tina, and they're not at all embarrassed being grown-ups at this kids' dance. Mom's dancing like I've never seen her dance before and part of me is embarrassed, but part of me is proud that she's so cool.

I sing "Thank You" by Dido, and Rick attempts the rap version by Eminem right after it to change tempo, then "You Got it Bad" and "Nice and Slow" by Usher. I love singing "Like a Pill" by Pink, and "Will You Still?" by Coo B6. By now my nerves have totally gone—I'm in my shower and there's only me and these four guys who think I'm great and have something special to give. I can't let them down, so I sing and sing. Freddie's in the wings, her fists clenched, jumping up and down with excitement.

There's no space between songs and Rick goes straight into the next song, Velvet Revolver's "You've Got No Right."

While I harmonize with him, his face is twisted with pain, and I know he's singing about Jenny—"*She won't be coming back again*." Yet he shoots me a small smile and I know that, although he's in pain thinking about her, he's okay.

I glance at Larry, who seems lost in his own little world. He's stunning, and Rick and I stare with our mouths open as he lets rip...extending his soul through his fingers and into his guitar to show us all his "shine" and that his "lights" are on.

I glance down and see Miss Tina staring with pride

at Rick, and I see him grin at her, and I realize that I know nothing of the pain he's shared with her, that she's helped him endure.

The whole hall erupts as we all sing as hard as we can, and as my throat tenses, my face twists with passion. I'm singing for Jenny who *"won't be coming back again,"* and for everyone who has ever *"fallen apart on the inside,"* and on the outside, for that matter.

When we finish Rick speaks into the mic, "We'll be back in a while."

As the noise subsides I hear Jeff say in a loud voice, "Did you see her? She's the girl that I..."

Danny's standing right in front of me, right next to them, and when he hears Jeff, he punches him right in his mouth. Jeff falls to the ground, and Danny stands over him and says, "That's my sister; don't you ever say anything bad about her again." He balls his fists, ready to pummel him into the ground.

Donnie rushes over to him and tugs on his arm. "Enough, son. Leave him; he's not worth it. Don't get yourself in trouble because of someone like him, okay?"

The curtains are being pulled and they draw to a close in front of Danny standing up for my honor and groups of kids who are usually desperate to sit in the back row but who are suddenly desperate to be in the front row.

My thoughts are in a turmoil. Rick hugs me and

tells me that I'm "great," which makes me feel warm all over until the girl I saw earlier, with short cropped brown hair and wearing glasses, comes behind the curtain and slips her arm around him.

"You were fantastic," she says to me. "Rick has told me so much about you; he thinks you're amazing."

I don't know what to say because she should be my rival.

"Thanks," I say, meaning it, even though the sight of her with her arm around Rick hurts.

We go backstage and I can see Danny, Miss Tina, Mom and Donnie coming to meet us, their faces beaming. I throw my arms around Miss Tina and she holds me tight.

"My precious girl," she says, "I knew you could do it. I'm so proud of you. You were amazing, and truly *beautiful*," she says it slowly to make her point, and this time I hear her; I *really* hear her.

Mom coughs, and I realize she's probably feeling a bit left out. After all, I'm *her* daughter and she must be able to see the love between us.

Miss Tina says to Mom, "You must be very proud of her."

"I am," Mom says, and I look at her, knowing what pain she's endured herself, and I feel overcome with love for her, so I go and hug her, long and hard.

Danny says, "Mel, you were fantastic. I'm so proud of you. Hey, did you see me punch that creep on the nose?"

I grin and hug him. I'm so glad he's my brother and I realize that something's changed between us over the past few weeks. He has stuck up for me, protected me, and shown openly that he's glad I'm his sister. I look into his face, as if I'm seeing him properly for the first time, and then I hug him again.

I go to the bathroom; Freddie comes with me and she's squealing with excitement.

"Mel, you were great, no, better than great, you were amazing. Did you see all those kids? Their mouths were gaping in awe. They couldn't believe it. Did you see them?"

"No, I was too scared. I didn't really look; they were a sea of faces. I pretended that I was in the shower."

"Well, you should've seen them. They just stood there...You should have seen their faces when their boyfriends were all staring at you. I couldn't help it, Mel...I laughed. It was funny."

I smile at her. I can't believe that she's talking about me. I've never had any effect on anyone before, except perhaps Rick, but that's only in a brother-sister way. No one has ever stared at me in the way she's describing. And certainly no girl has ever felt jealous of me enough to nudge their boyfriend in the ribs because he was paying attention to me.

She's jumping up and down with excitement and pushes me out of the bathroom to join Mom, Donnie and Miss Tina, who look excited and happy. Danny's waiting for us and he asks Freddie if he can stay in the wings with her for the second half, and she says "Yes." We hang out for half an hour backstage while the kids dance to a DJ, and it's good to see Julie, Tammy and Paul again. It seems ages since we were all together at Beach Haven.

Rick's on the stage messing around with his guitar and he calls me, "Mel, it's time, c'mon."

Miss Tina goes with Mom and Donnie and the others back to the school hall, where they stand as my protectors and my greatest fans. I feel like my Self-Esteem Tree is protected by a shield of adult strength and faith, but something has changed in me, because even if they weren't there, right now, I think I'd still be okay. Three hours ago when I first realized that the end-of-school-year party was the gig we've been practicing so hard for, I panicked and didn't believe that I could stand in front of the bullies and sing; I really thought I'd freeze. But being surrounded by adults and kids who believe in me has changed something inside me; I find that I can sing, but it's more than that. I don't *just* sing, I shine.

That's it...it's the "shine" in Miss Tina's story. It's my "shine" that's made things different in this school hall. Yes, I can sing but so can lots of people, but what's made the bullies stop and look at me and take me seriously is my "shine." I'm still me but I'm giving off something different towards the kids, and they're responding differently to me.

I go back onto the stage and take my place.

"Are you all right?" Rick asks. "Are you holding up okay?"

"Yes, I'm fine."

"Great to see Miss Tina and the others."

"Yes," I say, as the curtains open.

Everyone is waiting for more, a sea of faces, not one with any animosity towards me anymore. I smile at them and give them a little childish wave with my right hand. I can see my mom laugh and say something to Miss Tina, who laughs as well.

They start yelling, and as I hear them I feel as if my blood is coursing around my body twice as fast as it should be. But rather than be terrified, I'm excited and enjoying myself. We launch into the second half and I sing, jump and dance to Justin Timberlake's "Rock Your Body."

As we play on through the next hour, everyone's dancing. Occasionally I see a group of kids looking up at the stage pointing, not believing that the person they're looking at is none other than the ugly nerd in the front row of class, but they're not laughing anymore. I'm so engrossed in the music we're making that they fade from my consciousness, and the only important thing to me is the sound we're creating between us...it has a life of its own. I sing on and on, and time slips away.

There's movement in the wings and I glance over to see what's happening. It's the principal, and he's come to tell us that we have to stop because the evening's come to an end. Rick goes over to him while we stand there frustrated that it's over so soon, because we all want this moment to go on forever and ever.

I don't know what to do, as Rick hasn't told me what he's going to play for the last number. He beckons to Freddie and then he goes to the front of the stage and holds his hands out, expecting that everyone will be quiet, and they are. I imagine he's going to say that the principal has told us to stop, but I'm wrong; I'm more wrong than I can ever be.

Rick clears his throat.

"This party is in honor of you all having finished your school year, and we all know how much effort that takes, yeah?"

They cheer loudly.

"Well, we don't only learn about geography and history, or mathematics and English, we learn a lot more, and this last song is dedicated to the person who has taught me a whole lot about myself, and has been there for me this year through a tough time. She's amazing and is one of my best friends...I hope you value her for who she is."

He coughs to clear his throat and raises his voice slightly.

"*And* you need to make a stand right now, because she is so talented that everyone of you will want to know her when she's famous, which she will be. And on that day, you, you who have given her a hard time, will long to know her and be remembered as her friend."

He turns his back on the silence in the hall and takes my hand to lead me to a tall barstool that Freddie has just put in the center of the stage. He tells me to sit on the stool, and as I sit with my hands clasping my knees, I stare at him, wondering what he's going to do; I feel anxious and a bit embarrassed.

He turns around while I sit on the stool, my knees clenched in trepidation and he goes back to the mic.

"I'm going to sing, 'A Jewel Along the Way' by Jono Johnson, because that's what Melody is, a jewel along the way."

My stomach lurches as Larry, nerdy Larry, brings his guitar alive and makes it whine. No one's dancing, it's too breathtaking, and all the girls are staring at him, seeing him differently despite him being the same as he's always been.

The drummer hammers out his presence as Rick starts to sing, and all the time his eyes are on me and I am locked into his gaze. It feels as if there's no one else in the school hall.

I lost my soul the day she died,
They don't know how hard I tried
To hold her from the icy sea
And pull her back alongside me.

Rick frowns and I know he's singing about Jenny drowning, and how guilty he feels. My heart hurts for him. We haven't practiced this. Then it dawns on me that they've done it when I haven't been with them; they've done it for me. I'm overcome and I can't stop the tears from flowing down my face as he sings the next verse.

I watched her face sink deep below,
"Grab my hand, don't let me go,"
Yet in her eyes I saw the blame,
She disappeared; I cried her name.

Out of the corner of my eye I see Miss Tina watching him with pride.

They all start singing together.

"Grab my hand, don't let me go,"
Hear my pain, oh, don't you know,
Take my hand, I love you so.
Feel my pain, I miss you so.

He looks at me with a mixture of love in his eyes and pain on his face.

Blame, it ate me from inside
Leaving me no place to hide,
Can't they see my heart's in pain
Causing me to go insane?

They all sing together again.

"Grab my hand, don't let me go,"
Hear my pain, oh, don't you know,
Take my hand, I love you so.
Feel my pain, I miss you so.

Rick looks at me, winks and smiles, and then sings again.

Why was no one there for me,
No one there to set me free?
But then a jewel arrived one day,
Held my hand and I was saved.

Then something happens. It's Larry, it's unbelievable. He makes all his notes flow into each other, into an earth shattering blast of saying how it is, saying how pain is, how love is and how life is. I've never heard anything so powerful, so sexual, so moving, or so consuming; he makes my heart soar and die at the same time. He blasts the entire school hall out as his guitar screams with haunting pain, and everyone just stands and stares with their mouths open. He plays as if he's possessed by something wonderful, as if he's in heaven with his guitar, showing me his soul and everything that makes him who he is, and something pulls me towards him.

It lasts thirty seconds yet it's a lifetime to me, a

journey where I leave one Melody behind and become another. There's no going back; he's beyond words, and his playing is beyond words. How could I ever have thought that Larry was a nerd? He is the most amazing human being I know, and he's only fifteen. I can't believe it, and as he makes his guitar howl, which circles the hall and leaves us all shocked, Rick starts singing again.

Then a jewel, she took my hand,
Took me to a promised land,
She made me smile and made me play,
She is a jewel along the way.
She is the jewel who took my hand,
Took me to a promised land,
She makes me smile and makes me play,
She is a jewel along the way.

Rick's smiling at me and I can see in his eyes that he does love me; he says that I'm a jewel along the way, his jewel along the way. I smile back...he's wonderful. I love him. He saved me; I'd be dead if it weren't for him.

Larry snatches my attention again as he sedately, but powerfully, walks his fingers down the frets in a breathtaking display of his "shine" as Rick finishes singing.

Larry's "shine" is going crazy, it explodes on the stage and everyone is silent, not dancing or anything, not even trying to make out. They're just standing there with their mouths open. I can't believe the noise. All the boys in the band start playing at once and the noise and power is deafening; I clasp my hands over my mouth to stifle the scream of exhilaration inside me. It's monumental, huge, amazing, and I fear that I might die with the ecstasy of it all.

As all the guys in the band come to a crescendo, there's only one person I can look at—Larry—and there's something in his face that makes my stomach flip. I look at him and I'm dumbfounded. He's the boy that I was unkind to; his spots made him nerdier than me, yet as he makes his guitar become an extension of his soul, I know exactly what Miss Tina means about the "shine." He has it; I have it, and her story about physical features meaning very little when in the presence of the "glowing orb" around us rings in my head, along with Larry "shine." It's self-esteem and confidence that makes someone beautiful or handsome, and the sparkle of a person's "shine" is what makes them attractive.

The music closes in upon me—a raw, velvet, vibrant blanket—as I sit on the pedestal and feel like a million dollars, tears running down my face, tears of joy, not sadness...tears of wonderment. I can feel the stage vibrating, for the noise is phenomenal when all four boys sing and play as they come to the end.

The kids barely wait for them to finish before the whole hall erupts; they're going mad, hooting and hollering, shouting "more" over and over. But Rick and Larry both put their guitars down and step towards me. I have tears in my eyes but I'm not crying anymore...I'm ecstatic. They both hug me and Rick shouts in my ear, "Love you, babe," while Larry still holds on to me.

"Mel?" he shouts above the din, and I look into his brilliant, sparkling blue eyes that reflect his "shine." And suddenly there's only us in the room as he lowers his face to mine and kisses me; my first *real* kiss in front of hundreds of kids...and my mom!

The kids are still yelling and I look at them, feeling flushed, knowing that they'll all want to be my friend, now that they think I'm cool, but I remember Miss Tina's story about the little shepherd girl. I smile at them and wave, but I know that my "purse" is safely shut to all those who only want me for something other than just being myself. Then I look back at Larry, who's holding my hand, and I know that he's the guy in the tavern, the one that was hidden from view but who wanted the little shepherd girl for who she was and not for what she could buy. I can see how special he is, and his eyes tell me that I'm special to him, too.

The kids continue to yell for more, but I'm oblivious to them as Larry kisses me again. My heart is pounding, and I giggle as Rick smiles at us, knowing that my "purse" is open to those who love me—open, but safe.

About the Author

Dr. Celia Banting earned her Ph.D. by studying suicide attempts in adolescents and developing a risk assessment tool to identify those young people who may be at risk of attempting suicide. She identified several risk factors which, when combined, could increase the likelihood of an individual attempting suicide. Rather than write "how to" books or text books to help teenagers cope with the risk factors, Dr. Banting has incorporated therapeutic interventions into novels that adolescents will be able to identify with. These novels are designed to increase the adolescents' ability to take care of themselves, should they have minimal support in their families.

Dr. Banting's career has revolved around caring for children in a variety of settings in both the United Kingdom and the United States. She is dedicated to helping troubled children avoid the extreme act of suicide.

WIGHITA PRESS ORDER FORM

Book Title	Price	Qty.	Total

I Only Said I Had No Choice
ISBN 0-9786648-0-9 $14.99 x _____ $_____
   Shane learns how to control his anger and make positive life
   choices; and he gains understanding about adult co-dependency.

I Only Said "Yes" So That They'd Like Me
ISBN 0-9786648-1-7 $14.99 x _____ $_____
   Melody learns how to cope with being bullied by the in-crowd at
   school and explores the emotional consequences of casual sex.
   She raises her self-esteem and learns what true beauty is.

I Only Said I Couldn't Cope
ISBN 0-9786648-2-5 $14.99 x _____ $_____
   Adam learns how to deal with grief and depression. He works
   through the grieving process and explores his perceptions of
   death and life.

I Only Said I Didn't Want You Because I Was Terrified
ISBN 0-9786648-3-3 $14.99 x _____ $_____
   Hannah experiences peer pressure to drink alcohol. She learns
   about teenage pregnancy, birth, and caring for a new baby.
   Hannah faces the consequences of telling lies and learns how to
   repair broken trust.

I Only Said I Was Telling the Truth
ISBN 0-9786648-4-1 $14.99 x _____ $_____
   Ruby embarks upon a journey to rid herself of the damaging
   emotional consequences of sexual abuse.

Sub Total $_____

Sales Tax 7.5% ($1.13 per book) $_____

Shipping/handling $_____
1st book, $2.50; each add'l. book $1.00 / U.S. orders only.
(For orders outside the United States, contact Wighita Press.)

TOTAL DUE $_____

PLEASE PRINT ALL INFORMATION.

Customer name: _____

Mailing address: _____

City/State/Zip: _____

Phone Number(s): _____

E-mail address: _____

**Make check or money order payable to Wighita Press and
mail order to:** P.O. Box 30399, Little Rock, Arkansas 72260-0399
Look for us on the web at: www.wighitapress.com   (501) 455-0905